ALWAYS A LITTLE FURTHER

Always a Little Further

*A classic tale of camping, hiking and
climbing in Scotland in the thirties*

by
ALASTAIR BORTHWICK

Diadem Books · London

First published by Faber, London, 1939
Second Edition published by Eneas Mackay, Stirling, 1947
Republished (photoreprint) by John Smith, Glasgow, 1969
Republished (photoreprint) by Diadem Books, London, 1983
Republished (photoreprint) by Diadem Books, London, 1989
Reprinted 1993

All trade enquiries to:
Hodder and Stoughton, Mill Road, Dunton Green, Sevenoaks, Kent

British Library Cataloguing in Publication Data:

Borthwick, Alastair
  Always a little further. – 5th ed.
  1. Scotland – Description and travel
  I. Title
  914.11'04858   DA867

  ISBN 0-906371-08-2

Printed and bound in Great Britain by
Biddles Ltd, Guildford and King's Lynn

To
HAMISH
who started
it all

No character in this book is
fictitious

CONTENTS

INITIATION

PEOPLE

CLIMBS AND CROSSINGS

Master of the Caravan

But who are ye in rags and rotten shoes,
You dirty-bearded, blocking up the way ?

Ishak

We are the Pilgrims, master ; we shall go
Always a little further . . .

JAMES ELROY FLECKER :

Hassan.

CHAPTER ONE

ENTER HAMISH

I

ARROCHAR is not a beautiful village at the best of times ; but on this particular Saturday afternoon in 1933 trippers had added to its normal air of untidiness. A steamer had disgorged several hundreds on to the pier and was pounding down Loch Long for more ; a squadron of empty 'buses was drawn up outside the principal hotel, awaiting passengers whose attention was divided between high teas and beer ; and the local ice-cream merchant's barrow was besieged. A tinker with bagpipes blasted his way along the water-front, followed by a small and rapacious daughter extorting pennies. Sandwich papers littered the shore where groups of women, by sheer force of character making this alien spot a Glasgow park, alternately ate, gossiped, and turned to scold the children who sought crabs among the rocks. The dominant smell was equal parts of salt sea, dusty tar, and petrol.

But Arrochar, for all its air of cheap bustle, could not conceal the fact that it existed on the fringe of tripper-land, that it was an outpost among the resorts dotted about the Firth of Clyde to cater for the week-ends and summer holidays of Glasgow. The bustle was confined to a narrow strip along the shores of Loch Long. Above and beyond were mountains, scarcely touched by the tide-mark of humanity at their bases, impervious to pipers and ice-cream barrows or to the customers of either, as aloof and untouched as the desert which hems in the airport of Timbuctoo.

Through the crowds by the pier John and I walked slowly, saying nothing and trying to accommodate our minds to the idea that we were not alone. We watched perspiring women weigh themselves on penny-in-the-slot machines, and heard the cheerful hubbub of Glasgow enjoying itself. We saw children, saved from the wheels of 'buses, being spanked out of hand in sheer relief. People noticed our rucksacks, and cried, " Aw, the hikers ! " and to these people we smiled ; but neither of us spoke until we had bought ice-cream and sat upon the sea-wall to eat it.

" This," said John, " is very unfortunate."

It was. The little camping we had done had been done near Glasgow ; and for this, our first ambitious excursion on our own, we had tried to select a quiet district off the main tourist and tripper routes. Arrochar had looked quiet on the map. And here we were. We fell silent again while we ate our ice-cream, watched 'bus after 'bus spew forth its cargo, and wondered if anywhere in the district there was a camp site beyond earshot of bagpipes and squalling infants. Depression settled on us as on an Everest expedition which, having turned along the wrong glacier, finds itself on Brighton Pier.

" I don't think much of that either," said John, waving a hand towards the far shore of the loch, where a mile of tents cluttered up the roadside ; " wife-beating and harmoniums till two in the morning, I'll be bound."

Above the distant strip of tents rose Ben Arthur,

a mountain commonly called the Cobbler even by
those, and I am one, who have never been able to
see the slightest resemblance to a cobbler in any of
the three crazy pinnacles which cap it. A devious
road wound along the loch shore, lapped on one side
by the water and on the other by the grey-white froth
of tents. Above rose steep, bracken-covered slopes
which, tiring in their upward sweep, gained strength
on a level shelf of ground before soaring once more
to the three pinnacles which lurched across the skyline.
It was a striking mountain. We were distracted by
many more immediate and noisy features of the
landscape, but always we were drawn back to it and
to the high, level shelf cut into its side. We began
to look at it thoughtfully.

" I suppose we *could* get a tent up there," said John
at last in a way which suggested that he had his doubts.

We considered this.

" Why not ? " I asked.

John looked at the Cobbler and then at his
rucksack, weighing the angle of one against the bulk of
the other, and both, it seemed, against the heat of
the sun. He smiled.

" Come on," he said, and swung his rucksack on to
his shoulders.

At five o'clock we left the road and started up
the left bank of the burn which drains the Arrochar
face of the Cobbler. The afternoon was excessively
hot, and the weight we were carrying was ludicrous.
We had yet to learn that heavy pots and pans, thick
ground-sheets, raincoats, and much tinned food are
luxuries to be avoided upon a mountain, just as we
had yet to learn that there was an excellent path on the

far side of the burn. On our bank, bracken grew with
the abandon popularly associated with *machetes* and
tropical jungles, and in some places was taller than we
were ourselves. Forcing a passage through it while
carrying a heavy rucksack up a steep slope was trying.
Also, there were flies. The first thousand feet was a
purgatory of heavy breathing, sweat, and the forlorn
beauty of bracken fronds against the sky ; but higher
up the bracken thinned. We cast ourselves down
on a bank of heather and bog-myrtle, propped our
shoulders against a rock, and looked down on Loch Long,
where cars crawled along the road and a steamer
unloaded another ice-creamless multitude. The sun
was still very hot, and the air reeked with the tang of
bog-myrtle against a background of other mingled
and satisfactory smells. Sounds were faint and
Arrochar distant. Everything was remote, peaceful,
and unreal.

Suddenly a commotion arose among the crowds
on the pier. They parted and put forth a white figure
which shot from the edge of the pier, poised for an
instant in mid-air, and began to drop gracefully towards
the water.

It is strange, now, to look back and realise that
I wondered who the diver could be, that in those days
I did not know any one who would cast himself from a
pier at low tide for no other reason that that it was
Saturday, with the city fifty miles away and the rush
of warm air on downward face a joy. It is strange,
too, to realise how much " in character " Hamish
was that first time I saw him, strange because now the
incident takes its place at the end of a long perspective
of incidents which give it a relevancy it did not possess

at the time. . . . Hamish on the Crowberry Ridge, with sleet whipping across the streaming hand-holds, eighty feet of air below his boots and battle in his eye; Hamish hanging over a map, tracing out some fantastic route and scoffing at the doubters—" Och, don't be daft, man. Of course, it's possible ! " Hamish in Dan Mackay's barn, arguing with tramps ; Hamish on his preposterous motor-bike ; Hamish in the Chasm ; Hamish the eternal optimist, tingling with excitement in a dozen situations when a plot was on foot and enthusiasm in the air.

All these things were latent in the tiny figure poised above Loch Long ; but we watched with only mild interest as the dive ended and he clipped out into the open water. The seaward edge of the pier was black with spectators, who, judging by the noises which reached us, were either shouting encouragement or expressing disapproval. Disapproval was the more likely, because the loch was nearly a mile wide and the little figure did not turn back until he was more than half-way across. There was a momentary revival of interest when he scrambled up the shore, and then attention turned to other things. John and I plodded on uphill.

We did not pitch our tent until nearly eight o'clock, and even then did not reach the level ground, though the sun was less hot and the going easier. We were unused to carrying loads, and when we came on two enormous boulders and a level patch of ground beside the burn, we stopped. Twenty minutes later we had the stove going. The tent door faced the summit. The three pinnacles were gigantic fingers, black against the sunset. Nothing stirred. Arrochar and all its works were out of sight below the skyline, and there was silence.

We lay by the tent door and took it all in.   We had heard that an easy path led to the top of the central peak by a circuitous route hidden from our sight ; but it was difficult to believe that any route to it could be entirely easy, for the cliffs appeared to be sheer and we did not then know that the Cobbler's goods are all in that shop window which faces Arrochar. However, when we had shared half a pound of sausages and four eggs, all things seemed possible. We lay back and, having disposed of any difficulties we might encounter on the following day, fell into a pleasing conversation of which self-congratulation was the chief part. We had done well to carry our gear so high, against such fearful odds of heat and flies, and through bracken whose clogging qualities were certainly unsurpassed in the length and breadth of Scotland. We were very fine fellows. We were agreed on that.

" I wonder if any one has ever camped up here before," said John.

" I'd be surprised if any one has," I said with simple pride. There was no doubt about it. We were very fine fellows indeed.

For the length of time it takes to clean two greasy plates with a handful of heather there was silence. Then a yodel came rolling over the mountainside from some point below us. There seemed to be voices, too. This was scandalous. I shouted " Hallo ! " once ; and immediately came the answer, a loud yodel with a trill at the end of it. Three people struggled over the skyline and walked towards us.

The first was a lad with a dark, lined face and the

head of a Pict ; the second a neat, quiet-looking girl who contrived to appear well-dressed with whipcord breeches on her legs and a climbing-rope round her shoulders.

" Yo-de-lay-i-do ! " said the third, who was Hamish, an amiable creature in his early twenties, with a little black moustache, a tall and well-built body, and a truly tremendous grin. " What on earth are you camping here for ? You'll get washed out if it rains. There's a far better site higher up."

We said we did not know the mountain, and had taken the first site we could find.

He cocked an eye at the sky, and announced that we should probably be all right. " The good weather's going to hold," he said, and beamed upon us so paternally that we began to feel five years old.

" You're rock climbers, aren't you ? " I asked.

" Sure," he said. " Sure, we're rock-climbers. A great game. Absolutely great. Sticking out a mile. Super."

After which pronouncement he looked us up and down, not unkindly, and asked us if we climbed.

" No," I said, " we don't. But perhaps you can give us some advice. You see, we're going to Glenbrittle, in Skye, next month with two other lads. Just to do a little walking, you know, with maybe an odd day on the hills. And we don't know much about the place, and . . ."

An expression of blank incredulity was spreading over Hamish's face. " An odd day on the hills ? Walking ? *Walking ?* Good Lord ! " He turned to the others. " They're going to Skye to walk ! Look here," he said, turning to us, " What's your name ? "

I told him. "And this is John Boyd," I said.

"And I'm Jimmy Hamilton, but everybody calls me Hamish. And that's Tizzie Frame, and that's Murdo Stewart. Now, look here, Alastair, the finest rock-climbing in Britain . . . maybe in the world . . . is right on your doorstep at Glenbrittle. It would be absolutely criminal to go there and walk. My goodness, if you . . ."

"Hamish! Don't bully the man!" said Tizzie. She turned to us with an apologetic smile. "He gets a little enthusiastic, you know."

I chuckled. I had not met such a restless mass of enthusiasm before, and the man was evidently only warming to his subject. He was like the first stages of an eruption. Murdo sat laughing on the heather, enjoying the performance hugely.

"Well, don't overdo it," said Tizzie. "Maybe he doesn't want to climb."

"Of course, he wants to climb!" said Hamish scornfully. "Now, look. You can buy boots for twenty-five bob. A hundred-foot rope costs a quid. And here! When did you say you were going to Skye? Next month? The beginning of September? Great! I'll be there then. I'll see you right when you arrive. Where are you staying—the hostel? Fine! So am I."

"So it's all settled," said Murdo, grinning from the heather. "Whether Alastair likes it or not, it's all settled. Hamish, how often have I told you that you can't go molesting strangers like that?"

Hamish deflated a little. "Well, it was a good scheme, anyway," he said. "Sorry. Eh . . What are you doing to-morrow, you two?"

John looked him squarely in the face. "We're *walking* up the Cobbler," he said.

"Not on your life you're not!" said Hamish, reviving. "Not on your life you're not! You're coming with us. Aren't they, Tizzie?"

"Seriously, I think you'll enjoy it," she said. "Do come."

"We won't kill you," said Murdo. "We're not so daft as we look, and that demented soul over there really is a surprisingly good climber. It's at least worth a trial. What d'you say?"

I looked at John. John looked at me.

"Thanks," I said. "We'll come."

We said good-night and they turned uphill to pitch their tent; but, as they left, a sudden thought crossed my mind.

"Hamish," I said, "did you by any chance have a bathe this afternoon?"

"Now, it's funny you should ask that," said Hamish, "because I did have a little swim."

We watched them out of sight. It grew dark. Far into the night we heard a mouth-organ playing below the cliffs of the Cobbler.

II

A precipice, seen by a person who has never had to climb one, is a sadly misunderstood part of the landscape. It is written off, in the mind of the beholder, as so much light and shade set at an angle of ninety degrees to the part of the world where reasonable men may walk, a given area of rock, steep as a wall and

impossibly smooth. It is seen as a whole, because
no sub-division seems possible.

In just such a way might a savage examine a map,
and, finding on it no pictures he could understand,
discard it as a thing without form or significance.
Roads, rivers, and pathways would be, to him,
meaningless scribbles. There are many cliffs in Scotland
which reach a height greater than one thousand feet ;
but I know of none (except sea-cliffs, which by their
very nature are undermined and therefore tend to
overhang) which even remotely approaches the vertical
or could by any stretch of the imagination be called
smooth. The uninstructed man, like the savage,
cannot read. He does not know that this shadow
means a gully in which battleships could be sunk,
that that dip in the strata indicates a terrace wide as a
road, that that thin thread of darkness is a chimney
which may take a man in safety to the summit. The
scale is so vast and so far beyond his comprehension
that the conventional signs of the cliff mean as little as
those on the map. Therefore, if he should think of
rock-climbing at all, it is as a foolhardy sport clear
against the laws of God, man, and Sir Isaac Newton.

It was in this uninstructed state that we reached
the lowest rocks of the Cobbler. It was ten o'clock
on a perfect morning, and the sun must have been
making pretty play with the waters of Loch Lomond,
from this height visible through a gap in the hills.
It must have been so ; but I do not remember noticing
it, for my mind was filled with other things, such as the
breaking strain of Alpine rope, the gripping powers of
ordinary shoes, and the dubious state of my morale.
Even I could see that the ridge of the south peak which

we intended tackling was far from vertical ; but it was
steep enough. It rose in tiers of grassy ledges, linked
by abrupt little faces of rock, after the fashion of a
jerry-built staircase, and continued so to rise for four
hundred feet, at which point it tumbled earthwards in
one excessively steep and almost unbroken sweep.
In general outline it was not unlike a shark's dorsal
fin, and our programme was to climb up the long, easy
ridge and down the steep one.

" Some say the middleman's knot is best," said
Hamish, uncoiling the rope, " but I'd use a simple
overhand one if I were you. Like this. There. Now
get it over your shoulders and round your waist. That's
fine. You'll do."

John and I stood, clumsily and without enthusiasm,
like two sacks of grain waiting to be hauled into a
granary. I do not know what John was thinking or
feeling, but I know I was praying that I should not
disgrace myself. On the previous night this had not
troubled me unduly, for it has seemed to me that rock-
climbing was a sport in which a beginner might well
disgrace himself with honour ; but now, with a totally
unconcerned girl at my elbow, this argument did not
seem so convincing as it once had done. Tizzie was
talking about the weather. She was saying it was a
grand day. She was saying one met such nice people
on mountains. She was behaving as if she were
embarking on her second cup at a tea-party, and was
knotting the rope round her waist in the casual manner
of one cutting a slice of cake.

" There's going to be an awful crush on this rope,"
she said. " I think you'd better climb unroped,
Hamish. Murdo can lead."

Murdo led. He stepped off the heather on to a sloping shelf of rock, scrambled up it, and disappeared round a corner. The rope trickled after him slowly. It stopped, then suddenly began to move faster as he dragged in the slack.

"On you come, Alastair," he shouted.

Murdo took no chances, but kept the rope which linked us taut, so that if I had slipped I should have done no more than dangle. The shelf was easy ; but at the corner it ended in the way the earth was reputed to end in the days when it was thought to be flat. It just flopped. I know now that the drop was not a great one ; but then it seemed enormous, and I was glad to turn my back on it and grapple with a vertical rock on top of which Murdo stood, grinning encouragement.

"Take it easy," he said, " I've got you."

And then it came to me that he did have me ; that I was linked to him by a rope which, for all practical purposes, was unbreakable ; that I could let go, if I so desired, and come to no harm. The effect of this was curious ; but I believe it is an experience shared by most beginners. It was, simply, that the world, its worries, and its inhabitants ceased to exist, wiped clear from my consciousness ; and the only three realities left in the universe were myself, the small niche of rock which was the next handhold, and a passionate desire for union between them. I was not a human being suspended over a fifty-foot drop. The drop had vanished with the rest. I was an animal, exercising all its muscle and guile in an attempt to place five fingers on three inches of rock, thought and action bent on one object to the exclusion of all others, like a cat stalking a bird. In time (though there was no such thing as time) the handhold gave way to another handhold, and another, and another. A pair of boots appeared level with my face. I pulled myself over the edge and sat panting. Murdo smiled at me, and automatically I smiled back. I turned, and looked over the edge. And then, and only then, did the gears re-engage and the world become the world again.

"Gosh!" I said, awed. "I came up that!"

After that we enjoyed ourselves. The strange, other-worldly, Alice-in-Wonderland feeling never quite left me at the difficult places; but it diminished as the day passed, and by the time we had reached the north peak John and I were able to sit with our legs dangling over the drop and agree with Tizzie that one met such nice people on mountains. The ground we had covered was easy; but we did not know that, for we had not yet learned that a vast amount of space below one is not of itself a difficulty, and that the difficulty in rock-climbing varies according to the presence or absence of holds. To us, the drop was everything, and we were enormously impressed by the feats of Murdo and Hamish, who, climbing either in the lead or ropeless, had little or no assistance to expect if they slipped. Neither of these gentlemen appeared to be at all put out by thoughts of danger. Murdo, steady and solid, climbed with the slow air of pleasure which men have when they are fed and have a pipe going well. Hamish, mercurial soul, careered upwards, yodelling as he slid from one ledge to the next, moving with a fluid grace which was pure cat. Escape from the city evidently meant much to him. He was brilliantly alive. His conversation was mainly

exclamatory, consisting of " Absolutely great !
Sticking out a mile ! Visibly projecting ! " and similar
pronouncements which meant nothing but expressed
animal high spirits to a degree I have seldom heard
equalled.   Tizzie shook a maternal head, half
sorrowfully, half in admiration.

" If he didn't get away climbing at the week-ends,"
she said, " he'd explode."

We reached the central peak by mid-day ; but
long before then the Cobbler had become a place of
pilgrimage, for Arrochar had a Youth Hostel, and
many of those who had slept there hoped to acquire
merit and a view from the painful grind to the summit.
At least twenty came from that quarter. The morning
bus yielded another dozen or so.   Nor were we the only
climbing party in sight.   The fact that we had camped
high had given us a start ; but from the summit of the
south peak we had seen two parties across the corrie
roping up for an assault on the north, and others were
before us on the central peak.   They crawled like flies
over the face of the Cobbler ; and it was not too fanciful
to imagine that the mountain might sigh in its sleep,
shake a rocky paw free of the heather blanket which
surrounded it, and brush the insects off.   To us, who
had imagined mountain tops to be uninhabited deserts,
it was surprising that there should be so much life in
this twisted landscape of rock.   Here was a society
whose existence we had never suspected.

We arrived at the top of the north peak in due
course and good order, though, thanks to the fact
that I wore shorts and John a kilt, with less skin on
our knees than we had had a few hours before.   The
mist had come down, and there was no view ; but

this was partly compensated for by the arrival of a dozen highly efficient-looking gentlemen with ropes, boots, and rich Glasgow accents, who appeared over the north shoulder and announced themselves as the Creag Dhu Mountaineering Club, out of Clydebank. Hamish knew them. John and I sat entranced while a stream of technicalities flowed between them. It appeared that not only had some one done the Right Angled Gully Direct and the Jug-Handle, but that Jock Direct would go although there was some very thin stuff and a shortage of belays at the top. On the other hand, the Ramshorn still would not go, although some one had had a shoulder from some one else on the bad pitch and had got busy on the turf overhang with a shovel. And Jock Nimlin thought the Recess Route would go direct. All this was delivered at speed and with great earnestness. At some parts Hamish looked grave, as if the Government had fallen ; other parts he greeted with a pleased chuckle. This climbing, it seemed, was a serious business.

The Creag Dhu Mountaineering Club departed and soon afterwards we followed. It had been a grand day. It seemed a pity to spoil it by dragging out the savour or tiring ourselves beyond appreciation. We turned to the tents and the evening bus, our brains buzzing with new people and new ideas.

John and I had led what are commonly called sheltered lives, which meant that in our world things still happened as we had been taught they would at school. And our school did not legislate for people like Hamish, or the Right Angled Gully Direct, or that extraordinary creature in the Creag Dhu who spent his week-ends hitch-hiking and sleeping under hedges, and who told us that the only way to make corduroy climbing breeches fit was to let them dry on you three times. The impact of these things and people on our minds was considerable. In the three years since we had left school, many things had happened to make us suspect that the world was a slightly less ordered and restricted place than we had been led to believe. But this was immense. This was so immense that it would have, as it were, to be taken home and assimilated slowly, item by item. It would have to be believed by degrees.

"Now, don't forget," said Hamish, as he, and Murdo, and Tizzie saw us on to our 'bus, "boots are twenty-five bob, and a rope's a quid."

The 'bus started to move. They waved.

"See you in Skye," shouted Hamish as we turned the corner.

CHAPTER TWO

HUNGER MARCH

I

SOME day a poet will do justice to the railway journey from Glasgow to Mallaig and end the matter once and for all. Until then it is a subject to avoid. The theme is noble, inviting a great heaping up of metaphor and adjective, a pen splashing purple ink, for it is the most beautiful journey in Britain ; but the pens of so many prose writers have splashed only an anæmic blue in its honour that I feel prose is unequal to the task. Let us say, simply, that the train arrived at Fort William, picked up Sandy Mackendrick from the platform he had reached by the through train from London, and continued on its way to meet the mid-day boat at Mallaig, Sandy was excited and a little puzzled. For a month he had been receiving relays of letters, couched in lyrical terms, on mountains and other matters which seemed remote to one who earned his living in London. What, he wanted to know, was all this about ? He had obeyed instructions and bought boots. He had joined the Scottish Youth Hostels Association. He had bought a rucksack. But why this sudden rabid enthusiasm ? And who was Hamish ?

So we told him all about it, chapter and verse, from Fort William to Mallaig, and from Mallaig by sea to Broadford, where we left the boat and set foot for the first time on the Isle of Skye. There were

four of us—John, Sandy, William Makins, and myself.
William was a tall youth whom few people ever seemed
to call " Bill." He had a high forehead and a weakness
for economics, and he was managing to maintain his
customary air of dignity despite the fact that he was
wearing a pair of breeches made for his uncle forty years
before, when cyclists, sartorially, were cyclists. These
objects had been resurrected for the occasion from
some obscure cupboard : he had seen our knees when
we returned from Arrochar.

Sandy and William had been friends since
childhood, and were utterly unlike in most respects,
as many such couples are. William argued from
precedent, Sandy from his own fertile ideas. William
was patient, Sandy impetuous. William saw a thing,
studied it, liked it, kept on liking it ; Sandy spent
his life in a hurricane of enthusiasms which died as
suddenly as they began. To this partnership, when
I joined it, I added much voluble and irrelevant
argument ; and John, who came to know us later,
contributed wit and the ability to pin down most of
the hares Sandy and I started. We were a curiously
assorted quartet.

We walked into a shop and bought post cards.

" So you are going to Sligachan ? " said the old
man we found behind the counter, a benign old soul
with a soft, liquid accent which flowed through a tangle
of white beard.

We said that that was our intention.

" Chust so," murmured the old man. " Chust so.
And what 'bus would you be catching ? "

The one that met the boat, we said.

" Dear, dear ! " The ancient was perturbed.

" Do you tell me that, now ! That is a fery great pity, indeed it is, a fery great pity. Why ? Because the 'bus did not bother to wait for the boat, and I doubt if you will get another one before nine o'clock."

" Just like that," I said. " It didn't bother to wait."

" No," said the old man.

We absorbed this information in silence. Then Sandy produced a map, started a council of war, and roped in the old man as an expert witness.

" It's four o'clock now," said Sandy, leaning over the map, " and we're here." He jabbed a finger at Broadford. " At nine o'clock a 'bus arrives and takes us north to Sligachan, here. Say it takes an hour. Ten o'clock. And after that we've to walk nine miles south-west in the dark to Glenbrittle, over a moor we've never seen in our lives, to a hostel where they go to bed at eleven. Not likely ! What's to prevent us cutting across country, and going north-west direct to Glenbrittle ? "

" And sleeping out," said John. " We have the tent ; but all the blankets bar one have been sent on ahead. Still, we could make do for the night."

" Sleep out by all means, if we need to," said Sandy, " but I don't see why we shouldn't walk right through the night and fetch up at Glenbrittle in time for breakfast. It doesn't look more than thirty miles at the outside, and I could do with some exercise. It's better than kicking our heels here for five hours, anyway."

" But," said William, " what's the path like ? "

" Road for ten miles or so, then a path," said Sandy. " Doesn't look too bad."

He looked at the old man for confirmation, and received an affirmative nod.

"Yes, yes," said the old man, "the path will be all right."

And so it was agreed, though our decision would have been different had we known two facts, first that in Skye everything "will be all right" because the natives are so polite that they will agree black is white rather than contradict a stranger ; and second that, thanks to the atrocious state of the path we had to cover, the journey could not be done in a single night. Two and a half days were to pass before we reached Glenbrittle ; and our total supply of food was eight sandwiches and a slab of chocolate.

II

We covered twelve miles that night, becoming increasingly conscious as each mile went by that our last square meal had been eaten on the train early in the morning, and that our chances of crossing the moor in darkness were slender. When, at ten o'clock at night, we reached the point where the road ended and the moor track began, we were ravenous and the night was so dark that we could not find the track. We did the only possible things. We pitched the tent and ate the sandwiches. It was a silent night, without wind. The sky was overcast, so that little of the ground was visible ; but there was still some light on the horizon, throwing one of the Red Hills into profile against the sky, a slope so straight that it might have been drawn with a ruler. In the foreground it was reflected in the shallows of Loch Slapin. And something told me that soon there would be frost.

At this stage it is necessary to describe the odd and inept collection of equipment which filled the rucksacks of the expedition, because it was our equipment as much as our sad lack of training which brought us to grief in the end. The loads we carried were enormous. We intended to stay in Skye for a fortnight and to climb all the time, first of all from Glenbrittle Hostel, and later from our tent, which we proposed pitching among the outlying peaks of the Cuillin. Both climbing and camping are wet games. They both involve ample reserves of clothing, for one cannot rely on drying wet clothes overnight in readiness for the next day, especially in camp. So our rucksacks were crammed with clothes, primus stoves, boots, a rope, a tent, and much else besides, to the tune of forty pounds apiece. The only things they did not contain were the two vital ones—food and blankets. Food had not seemed necessary, and the blankets had been sent on ahead. In John's rucksack was one small travelling-rug, and in William's two-thirds of a ground-sheet, an ancient thing, pock-marked as the face of the moon, with threadbare patches from which the rubber had long since fallen.

We balloted for positions in the tent, which was a small affair designed to accommodate in comfort a maximum of two people. By this time the warmth of walking had left us, and a cold mist was creeping up from the loch. There is no warmth in sandwiches. We crammed on every stitch of clothing we had (William wore pyjamas on top of two full sets of clothes) and bedded down, shivering, like Babes in the Wood beyond the robin country. John and William had the inner berths, Sandy and I lay on either side of them, clutching the fringes of the rug, which was stretched taut as a drum. The mist was beginning to condense on the blades of grass by the door. An owl hooted. Somehow, we slept.

At four o'clock in the morning I woke, feeling as if I had been drowned and later revived by the primitive method of being rolled on a barrel. I was stiff, and sore, and miserably cold. Nor was my case unique, as I discovered as I stretched over to recover my end of the rug, stolen by Sandy in the night, for John spoke when he knew I was awake.

" This is awful," he said.

" Have you been awake long ? "

" Half-an-hour. And I'm getting colder and hungrier every minute. How much food have we ? "

" A sixpenny block of chocolate. But I think there's a village four or five miles away. Camasunary, it's called. It's on our way. We could get breakfast there."

William groaned and grunted his way to wakefulness.

" I feel like death," he said. " What was that about breakfast ? "

We explained.

" Camasunary ? Never heard of it. Anyway, there's a moon now, and anything's better than this ice-box."

We punched Sandy awake, ate all the chocolate, struck the tent, and started. We were stiff, and the start was painful. The owl still hooted. We lost the path almost immediately, and had to set a course across the moor by map and compass, stumbling in the moonlight through coarse grass and clumps of heather. But soon we were warm, and for a time saw the whole affair as a joke. We made quite good speed at that stage, laughing at the discomforts of the tent, and dreaming of ham and eggs at Camasunary ; but the way was rougher than we had anticipated, and our pace grew slower. By six o'clock it was light enough to walk with freedom, though the sun was not above the horizon ; but depression had set in again, and we were feeling sorry for ourselves. The moor was a bleak, monotonous grey, a level stretch of bog, and grass, and heather stretching endlessly in all directions, except that which lay ahead of us. There it tilted upwards a little, and beyond was the sky. A deep glen apparently lay beyond the rise.

Sandy was a hundred yards ahead, skirting a rocky bluff on the edge of the moor, when suddenly he shouted and began to run, an absurd little figure, all eagerness and joggling rucksack. He was wildly excited. He was cheering. We ran, too, and as we came round the bluff and looked out across the glen we stopped dead in our tracks and gaped. No one said anything.

The whole vast chain of the Black Cuillin, from Gars-bheinn to Sgurr nan Gillean, was stretched out like a curtain before us, with the sun, which had not yet dropped to our level, lighting the range from end to end. The mountains seemed close enough to touch. The morning mist was rising from them, softly, effortlessly, revealing first one buttress, then another, of the twenty peaks which stretched for miles, linked into a continuous whole by high ridges, scored by gullies, turreted, pinnacled, heaved up to the sky ; rock, rock, and more rock as far as the eye could see. And, Black

Cuillin or not, they were blue, the pale, delicate blue of a spring sunset, matt like a butterfly's wing. As the mist dissolved, more and more peaks took the skyline, more and more pinnacles broke the ridges, until only the gullies smoked. Then the last puff dissolved and broke, and they, too, were clear. The Cuillin were ours.

William began to sing. We slung on our rucksacks and lunged downhill to Camasunary.

III

We lay on an immense slab of rock, roasting in the sun and trying to snatch some of the sleep we had lost on the previous night. The sun was pitiless. All morning the heat had grown ; and now, at five o'clock in the afternoon when some respite might have been expected, it was worse than ever, for the sun was still high and the rock was releasing the stored heat of the day. Though, as Sandy pointed out, we were like four fried eggs in a pan, no escape was possible : at the place we had reached nothing grew. We were lost in a wilderness of bare rock which was hot to the touch.

William groaned at the casual mention of eggs. Eggs were a sore point. We did not talk about eggs. When we had reached Camasunary nine hours before in what we then imagined to be the last stages of hunger, we had found, not a village, but one house ; and the owner of the house had not relieved our hunger by frying ham and eggs, for the very good reason that he was not at home, and had locked the door behind him. We were, therefore, acutely conscious of the fact that our last real meal was thirty-three hours behind us, and our next one, to the best of our knowledge, thirteen miles ahead. We were lying on a wide terrace overlooking Loch Scavaig, hoping against hope that a small dot on the map, representing a spot three miles ahead, might be a house. Hoping was energy wasted. When we reached it, hours later, we found only scattered stones where a house had once stood. To eat, we had to reach Glenbrittle.

The view, from the point where we lay, was magnificent. Bare rock walls, on one of which we were perched, plunged down into Scavaig, a sea-loch. We were looking over and beyond it into the heart of the Cuillin horse-shoe, where naked cliffs sweep three thousand feet to the shores of Loch Coruisk, a fresh-water loch whose bed is far below the level of the sea. Still the butterfly blue dusted the rocks. There was no wind. Everything was calm, and vast, and still. And in the middle distance was a patch of gold and translucent green where the waters of Scavaig broke on a little beach. We looked at it. We looked at each other, and were unanimous. We should bathe.

But between us and the beach was the Bad Step, " on which," says the Scottish Mountaineering Club's Guidebook to the Cuillin, " there is not the slightest difficulty if crossed at the right place. Most people who get into trouble here attempt to cross too high up." Perhaps we tried to cross too high up. Perhaps we did hit off the proper route, but were too inexperienced, exhausted, and heavily laden for an easy passage to be possible. I do not know which of these alternatives is the true one, for in those days all of us had an exaggerated idea of the difficulty of the climbs we undertook, and none of us has seen the Bad Step since ;

but I do know that on that occasion the Bad Step lived up to its name.

To those who have confined their walking to England or the milder parts of the Highlands it may seem incredible that such a thing as the Bad Step can exist, for in these places there is never any natural difficulty which cannot be avoided without much trouble. If a boulder blocks the path, you walk round the boulder. If a river cannot be forded, you look for a bridge. But the Bad Step cannot be avoided : any one following the south-west coast of Skye from Loch Slapin to Glenbrittle must cross it. The wide, easy terraces which make progress along the wall above Scavaig a simple matter are cut by a great rock buttress which falls straight into the sea from a point high on the cliffs. Like much of the rock in the district, it is black and utterly smooth in outline, so that it looks like an enormous whale with its tail in the water and its head far up the mountainside. Two parallel cracks slant across its back, about five feet apart, for twenty or thirty feet ; and the only method we could devise, rightly or wrongly, for crossing it was to place our toes in the bottom crack and our fingers in the top crack, and shuffle. With forty-pound rucksacks dragging us outwards, this was exciting. Sandy was the only one to acquit himself well : he put on rubber-soled shoes and almost ran across it. I took twenty minutes, John and William gave it up altogether, toiled hundreds of feet up the mountainside, and crossed by a route which I suspect was considerably more difficult, thereby giving us the pleasure of watching them while we lolled at our ease, up to our necks in the sea and jeering the while.

We slept a little after that, basking like seals in the golden bay, subconsciously delaying the evil moment when we should have to move again. I have never seen a more barren spot. We might have been on a volcanic island, upheaved from the Pacific, a thousand miles from anywhere, so naked and deserted was the picture of green sea, black rock, and the filigree of gold dividing them. Scavaig was remote from the world. It was good to lie there in the sun: lying still, one did not feel so hungry.

But by six o'clock some sense of responsibility had penetrated to our sun-drenched minds, and we realised that further delay would mean another night in the open. This was unthinkable. During the afternoon the way had been so rough and the sun so hot that we had stopped every ten minutes, and to avoid this we now fell back on the ancient army plan of walking for fifty minutes in each hour. How we came to believe that we should accomplish this over the abominable acreage of rock stretching before us it is difficult to understand ; but believe it we did.

" Six-fifteen," said Sandy with great conviction. " Next stop, seven-five."

" Seven-five," we said, and meant it.

Five minutes later, still overloaded with pride and fine intentions, we came upon the brambles, a great, tangled bed of them, rich and fat and purple, contriving somehow to draw life from this howling wilderness. And they were ripe. We wavered and halted, but did not dare to drop our rucksacks. Sandy looked at his watch as if to assure himself that fifty minutes had passed, and seemed surprised when he found they had not. We all stood looking at each other,

and, casting sidelong glances at the brambles, attempted
to stem sudden and overwhelming springs of saliva.
Sandy cleared his throat nervously, and fiddled with a
tie which was not there.

" Eh . . . forty-five minutes still to go," he said
miserably.

I made a shameless dive.   The rest followed.

One hour later I drew away from the rest and sat
down pensively by the edge of the loch, purple to the
chin, feeling like the worst sort of Channel crossing,
and certain that to my dying day I should never eat
another bramble. Brambles are a snare and a delusion,
drawing blood with their thorns and giving worse than
nothing in return.   Brambles are all pip and no
nourishment.   Taken in bulk, and we had eaten pounds,
they settle in a cold mass and remain so, impervious
to the digestive processes of man.   The others joined
me.

" We had to eat," said John, " but that was a
mistake."

We sat gloomily, spitting pips ; and as we sat, the
sun dropped below the horizon and we knew that
we should not reach Glenbrittle that night.   It was
then that I discovered I had dropped the tent-pegs
as we crossed the Bad Step.

IV

Hunger will lead men to desperate expedients,
but we were not sufficiently desperate to touch the
villainous brew which John graced with the name of
breakfast.   He had, he said, thought of it as he dropped
off to sleep on the previous night.   The problem was

to render palatable our sole source of food, the bramble-patch beside the loch ; and in an attempt to solve it he had boiled on a wood fire (the primus, he discovered, had no paraffin in it) half a pound of brambles. He had found the wood on the beach. The result was revolting, and reeked of smoke. Had there been sugar to flavour the mixture we might have overlooked its appearance ; but without sugar that was impossible. It was of the consistency and bumpiness of the paste with which posters are stuck on hoardings, and was of a virulent purple which left the pot discoloured for weeks. I shook my head. I could not touch it. John ate one tentative spoonful and decided that the recipe was perhaps not such a good one after all. William embarked upon an elaborate discourse on the origins of Tyrian purple : the lost dye, he said, had no connection with boiled mussels as modern scientists claimed, but came from brambles gathered and boiled upon the beach of Scavaig. Sandy dumped the brew in the sea.

We were all hungrier than we had ever been in our lives : but we had slept well. Though the news that I had lost the tent-pegs had been greeted by groans, the accident was the best thing that could have happened, for it prevented us from erecting the tent. Instead we were forced to gather a pile of heather several feet deep and to spread the tent over it like a blanket. This bed, as well as being comfortable as a spring mattress, was really warm. Most of the cold in camp comes from below. The heather dealt so well with that, that the rug and tent were ample protection against the frosty night air. We slept in comfort for eight hours.

But hunger had become a serious problem. We had not eaten from plates for forty-eight hours, and even our miserable ration of sandwiches and chocolate was a memory of twenty-four hours ago. Glenbrittle was only eight miles away ; but by this time we had no illusions about either the nature of the ground or our own staying power. People have fasted for a month or more before now ; but they have taken care to do so at their ease, generally in glass cases at seaside resorts. They have not had to carry forty pounds over rough country with the temperature at seventy-five in the shade, a process which, we discovered, left the knees strangely weak.

The sun was as hot as ever. Any thought of walking for fifty minutes in each hour was unthinkable, for none of us could keep on his feet for more than twenty minutes without a long rest, and this despite the change which had taken place in the outlook of the party. Until the previous night the journey had seemed to us a glorified picnic, lightly undertaken and lightly to be carried out. In our innocence, which did not admit of starvation in civilized Scotland, we had taken no precautions and made no plans, thought nothing of our inexperience and lack of condition, but had muddled happily along, secure in the belief that, however unfortunate the start had been, we should reach Glenbrittle and food that night. We had bathed and slept, admired the view, argued, stopped when we felt inclined. But now we had learned our lesson, which was that we could not take liberties with a wilderness. There was nothing of the picnic about that final day, but a slow, determined grind towards Glenbrittle. Hunger, we discovered, was not the localized pain we had imagined it to be. Once our stomachs had abandoned hope of attracting food by the conventional distress messages they were wont to send out three times a day, they ceased to be the seat of hunger. We were hungry all over. Our finger-tips were hungry.

By noon we were walking on heather, on the lip of the cliffs where the southern Cuillin drop into the sea. The sea was a pale, transparent green, deep and abnormally clear. When we rested, we did so on the edge of the cliffs, and lay face-down, peering a hundred feet to the water and through it into green, silent under-water Cuillin where fish swam. There were seals, too, basking where the Atlantic swell broke against the cliffs; and sea-birds flung themselves like white stones at the water and the fish below. Southwards were the Inner Isles, Rum, Eigg, Canna, fading into a blue haze.

Sandy was the first to drop out. We were five miles from Glenbrittle on a steady, heart-breaking heather slope which dragged slowly to an upper moor. The slope was a mile long, and the heat was intense. Half-way up, Sandy dropped and refused to move.

" I just can't," he said, " I'm done. Leave me alone."

We said we could not leave him there.

" It's all right," he said ; " this will pass off. You carry on, and I'll follow when I'm able."

No one was feeling particularly noble. We took him at his word, and left him. As it happened, it was the best thing we could have done, because my turn came next, and Sandy had reached me before I recovered. We carried on together, and a few minutes later found William stretched out beside a burn. John, who held out until we reached the hostel, waited for us at the top of the rise, so that we finished together.

It was a curious experience, this feeling of weakness which suddenly took command of us. After more than two days of continuous heavy exercise, the brain and the body were functioning independently, so that the brain was left free while the body worked automatically. We were conscious, of course, that we were tired and hungry ; but misery appeared to have reached a level just above that which the body could endure and below which it seemed impossible to go. There seemed no reason, we thought, why this state of affairs should not continue in the same dull rhythm of planting one foot before the other for the few miles which remained. Yet suddenly and conclusively, within the space of half-an-hour, three of us knew that we could go no farther until we had gathered strength. It was mental rather than physical, for the reactions of our bodies were numbed. Nor was it an ordinary rest. We just sat down, and, having sat down, knew we could not get up. Our legs refused to support us, and half-an-hour passed in each case before it was possible to go on. I remember thinking how odd it was, as I lay too weak to move, that I had £9 in my pocket. It seemed all wrong.

We had not seen a living soul for two days, and were only a mile or two short of Glenbrittle when we did. We had all recovered, and were resting on the moor below Coire Lagan, an immense rock amphitheatre which opens into the mountains above Loch Brittle. I was lying, gazing idly at Sgurr Alasdair, which is the highest mountain of the Cuillin, pure rock and immensely sharp, when I thought I saw something move. The sky was clear blue and cloudless, so that the final razor-edge of ridge below the summit was thrown up in sharp relief. And as I watched I saw four tiny figures crawl out on to the skyline and scramble slowly to the top. I was excited. I was tired, and thirsty, and hungry ; but I still had it in me to be excited. We hoped to be up there soon.

Our imaginations broke all bounds on the final mile, and, nourished on starvation, reached heights of cruel and unwonted vividness. We thought of food so intensely that it seemed almost real. We took a delight in self-torture. Roast beef wrung my heart, roast beef slightly underdone, with Yorkshire pudding and thick gravy. The gravy, I insisted, must be thick, flowing round the rich brown flanks of roasted potatoes. What potatoes those were! They were real enough to touch, they and the French beans which lay beside them. Sandy swore he could smell the roast duck and green peas which filled his mind ; and John was haunted by a complete seven-course dinner.

"My lords, ladies, and gentlemen," he kept saying, "dinner is served."

We had not seen real food for nearly three days.

All this was rather pathetic, for our hopes exceeded our performance. We were too hungry to eat when we reached the hostel in the late evening. After a very moderate meal we tumbled into bed and slept for thirteen hours.

CHAPTER THREE

FOUR FOOLS RUSH IN

I STILL cannot understand why all four of us were not killed during that holiday in Skye. The one safe way to become a mountaineer is to learn behind an expert, letting him lead the difficult sections, so that you are always securely held by a rope from above until such time as you have acquired skill and discretion and are capable of leading easy climbs yourself. We did not have an expert leader. Hamish who had arrived a week earlier than we had done, had become friendly with a party of climbers whose skill equalled his own, and he spent his time with them, on difficult climbs. We had to work out our own salvation, bringing to bear on the problem that boundless ability for doing the wrong thing which made possible the events set out in the previous chapter. Our ineptitude had no limits. So ignorant were we of the rules of the game that not until long after the holiday was over did we appreciate most of the risks we ran. Only on one occasion were the risks such that even we could recognise them ; and then we were lucky to escape tragedy. Most of the time we muddled along, working by trial and error, happily ignorant of the fact that we were spending the most dangerous climbing days of our lives. We enjoyed it all enormously.

Our first day at the hostel we spent in bed, with frequent excursions to the kitchen to cook meals ; but on the second day we had recovered sufficiently to consult Hamish about a suitable climb. We found him darning socks beside the stove.

" Who's going to lead ? " he asked.

" I am," I said.

" Hum," said Hamish. " Well, it's like this. There are five classes of climbs in Skye—easy, moderate, difficult, very difficult, and severe. Easy is a walk. Moderate isn't much better. When you land on a difficult, you're getting somewhere. If *you* land on a very difficult, you won't get anywhere. And if you see a severe, raise your hat and walk past it." He paused, and inserted three thoughtful stitches in a sock. " Now, what we want is a nice easy-ish difficult, and that means the Window Buttress. Come here and I'll show you."

He led us to the door and pointed across the glen to Coire Banachdich, a slightly less extravagant hollow in the mountains than Coire Lagan, which we had passed on our way from Coruisk, but one which seemed to us sufficiently exciting for all that.

" See that long rib of rock with the gash in it ? " said Hamish, " that one on the right there, running up to Sgurr Dearg. Well, that's it. Just below the gash there's a hole right through the buttress . . . that's the Window . . . and beside the gash there's a dandy wee pinnacle. The guidebook talks about a seventy-foot vertical on the other side of the gash, but don't pay any attention to that. It's dead easy and nothing like vertical. You'll manage all right."

We thanked him, and prepared to go.

" Oh, and another thing," said Hamish, busy with his darning once more. " You'll be going to the top of Sgurr Dearg after that. It's just a scramble. But when you get to the top you'll find the Inaccessible Pinnacle. It's the actual summit of the mountain . . . a great thing . . sticking out a mile ! But you'd better be careful ; and if you do it at all, go up the east side. The west is the regular route, but it's not for little boys. I shouldn't try it, if I were you."

One hour later we had reached the foot of the rocks, and after another two hours were a short distance below the " dandy wee pinnacle," feeling pleased with ourselves, as we had every right to do, for the first section of the Window Buttress is not altogether easy. Immediately ahead was the Window, which was set at a point where two rock walls met at right angles, like the walls at the corner of a room. The Window was twenty feet up one of the walls ; and the problem was to climb through it. I found that it was not so easy as it looked, for the holds were few and small ; and, as the walls were vertical, I was out of balance and consequently straining my arms to hold my body in. However, there was a broad ledge below and it did not matter if I fell ; and there was also a heaven-sent hole in the rock about half-way up, a tiny cave with a level floor, where it was possible to rest. I found it an excellent spot in which to recover my breath. By levering myself upwards and inwards, I found I could get my head, shoulders, and upper body inside, with only my legs hanging down outside.

" Fine," I thought ; " and now I'll get on with the job."

There, however, was the rub. It was all very well to lever oneself into the little cave ; but it was the very devil to lever oneself out again, as any person who cares to dispute this statement will discover for himself if he lies face downwards on a table and then tries to get off it without using his feet. A good handhold inside the cave was essential if I were not to remain there for a very long time.

In the end I found the handhold ; but space was so constricted that some minutes passed before I could wriggle my fingers within reach of it and so escape. This was a small incident, and would have passed unnoticed if it had not been for the events which followed. John and Sandy came up without difficulty, sat down, and admired the view. I kept the strain on William as he came up, and admired the view as well. It was a fine view, wild and rugged ; but after a time it occurred to me that I had been admiring it for quite ten minutes, and that nothing very much seemed to be happening on the other end of the rope. Not to put too fine a point on it, nothing was happening.

" John," I said, " for goodness' sake have a look over the edge and see what William's up to."

John departed, and returned a minute later with a twinkle in his eye and the breath of a smile on his face.

" William," he said, solemnly, " appears to have his head in the mountainside."

He took the rope and left me free to direct operations from the edge. William was a sight worth seeing. The wall up which we had climbed was unbroken except by the opening formed by the mouth of the little cave, which was barely two feet square. This opening, however, was obscured by a monstrous excrescence which turned out to be the seat of William's forty-years-old breeches, suspended without visible means of support between heaven and earth, and sprouting a pair of waving legs. A muffled voice was demanding to be told how the blazes its owner could get out.

" There's a hold on the left-hand side, down about your waist," I yelled.

" I know there is, blast you ! " said the voice from the underworld, " but I can't reach it. My arms are too long. Whenever I try to move my hands down, my elbows stick out and jam. I'm here for life, I tell you."

" Well, we'll just haul you out on the rope. Stop jamming with your elbows and let yourself slide. We'll hold you all right."

" What ! " The voice was scandalized. " Dangle me on a rope ? " The voice then quoted from *Pygmalion*.

" Come on," I said quietly to John and Sandy, give me a hand. If we don't haul him out he'll be there a week."

They gave a hand. The first two heaves produced no result but yells from the bowels of the earth and violent agitation of the two legs ; but at the third, William swung into sight, clawing desperately at the lip of the cave, purple in the face, and dangling like Bruce's spider.

" You've missed your vocation, William," said Sandy, after we had hauled him up beside us ; " you're in the wrong job."

" And what," said William with heavy sarcasm, " would you suggest ? "

" Hind legs of the horse," said Sandy. " You'd make a fortune."

II

The mist came down as we left the Buttress for the broad shoulder of Sgurr Dearg, and grew thicker as we ascended. The boots of other climbers had left scratches on the rock, and these we followed for what seemed an interminable time over a jumbled maze of boulders, many of them big as cottages, which looked as if they had been scattered thickly from some giant's pepper-castor. Eventually we struck a narrow, serrated ridge, and followed it to the top of the mountain. Sandy, as usual, was ahead, and we heard him clamouring in the mist as something more than normally exciting came into his view. At first we thought he was announcing his arrival at the summit-cairn ; but that was not why he shouted. He had seen the Inaccessible Pinnacle.

The Inaccessible Pinnacle is one of the strangest freaks of nature in the Cuillin, where there are many strange things ; and, though it has been climbed thousands of times since the brothers Pilkington made the first ascent in 1880, it still looks as if it lived up to its name. Seen from the summit-cairn of Dearg it looks like a gigantic thumb, vertical or overhanging on all sides, and forty feet high. In actual fact, the fourth side, invisible from that angle, is far from vertical ; and it is up this long sloping edge that the easy route runs. We did not find the easy route, which was the one Hamish had advised us to take, until we revisited Dearg a year later. Dense, swirling mist not only made the Pinnacle seem twice the height it actually was and bemused what little sense of direction we had, but also hid the distant and easy route so effectively that we did not suspect its existence. We stood by the cairn in what Kai Lung would call a state of no-enthusiasm, with our respect for the brothers Pilkington growing every minute.

" And we mustn't go up the west side," said John. " Which *is* the west side ? "

" This side facing us," said William. " Or . . . no . . . wait a minute . . ."

We stood helplessly, dithering. The mist drifted in heavy patches which muffled sound and blotted out all landmarks.

" What do you think ? " asked Sandy.

" Blessed if I know," I said. " I *think* it's the side we can't see. If that's right, then this must be the easy side here."

"Doesn't look very easy to me," said Sandy ; but he tied on the rope and prepared to lead the climb at a point which, at a conservative estimate, was a hundred feet from the start of the easy route. He scraped dejectedly round the base of the Pinnacle, which overhung slightly. " Can't even get started," he said.

After five minutes of heaving and gasping, he had worked round on to a series of sloping ledges on the wall, which seemed to overhang. It looked impossible ; but the nailmarks led that way. The mountain fell away on that side, so there was a big drop below him.

" This is pig of a place," he said. " Rock's all slippery. But I think . . . I think . . . that if I manage the next bit I'll be all right."

He sounded unhappy, which was understandable, for all the holds sloped outwards, and the rock was basalt, a smooth rock, greasy when wet, unlike the rough, honest gabbro which predominates in the Cuillin. It was the sort of place where an even moderately experienced climber might have felt at home, but this was Sandy's first day on any mountain. The Inaccessible Pinnacle was one of our stupider mistakes. However, Sandy got up. He had a struggle, but he got up. I followed, and was thankful for the rope. John and William, having had an opportunity of watching and listening to our ascent, decided to admire what view there was from below, for dusk was approaching and there was no saying how long we should take to climb down.

Then the mist parted. First a long tunnel appeared, as if an arm had been thrust obliquely downwards into the mist from the Pinnacle, and left clear air where mist had been. I have not seen such a thing since. It was like looking through the wrong end of a telescope with walls, not of black, but of swirling grey ; and at the end, remote and strangely small, was a tiny lochan surrounded by rock and lit a ghastly green by some trick of the setting sun. The mist closed in again. William shouted. We turned, and saw the mist to the west thin gradually, so that the whole Minch, with the Outer Isles a narrow strip beyond, faded up like a photograph under developer and faded out again as softly as it had come. North, south, east, west, the mist drew aside momentarily, sucked into view a framed picture, and passed on with the picture under its cloak. After a time there were no more pictures. The mist settled, thick as ever.

"Will you come down last ? " asked Sandy.

I said I would. He had done his share by leading

the climb ; and there was always the chance that I could hitch the rope round a projecting rock and so lower myself to the ground. I held Sandy from above until he was safe, and then started down the route we had ascended. There was a projection which made a sound hitch, though I, not knowing that it had been used as such by three generations of climbers, was certain that it would collapse. At this stage we made our next mistake. An excellent method, known on the Continent as *abseil* and in this country as roping off, has been perfected for descending such places. The rope is hung round the projection so that both ends hang down to the ground. Then the climber wraps the double rope round his body in a complicated manner (there are several schools of thought about this part of the proceedings) and slides down to the bottom. The secret of the *abseil* is that the rope passes under one thigh and up over the opposite shoulder, so that the climber is actually sitting on the rope while he is sliding down it. The friction caused by this and other wrappings is so effective a brake that on some occasions the climber has to pull himself downwards. Once he is down, the rope is flicked free.

But this, of course, might never have been invented so far as we were concerned. It was just one more thing we had never heard of. My idea of descending the Inaccessible Pinnacle at a speed less than that of gravity was to tie myself to one end of the rope, pass the slack round the projection, and throw the other end down to Sandy, in the ill-founded hope that he might be able to lower me to the ground, using the projection as a pulley. The rope, naturally, jammed. That was to be expected. I still feel, however, that it might have chosen a happier time to do so than the precise moment when I reached the sloping mantelshelf which was the worst part of the climb. The wretched " pulley " was not even directly above me : it was about twelve feet up and ten to one side, so that if I did come off I was going to pendulum. I had to kneel on the sloping ledge, let go with both hands, and tug the rope until I had enough slack to allow me to move. And half-way through this delicate operation the mist lifted once more and John saw the sunset.

John admired the sunset, and said as much.

" Look at that red cloud ! " he said, moved.

I tugged the rope and gained an inch.

" And the yellow, William, the yellow ! All the Outer Isles . . . I suppose that's Barra over there . . . and the glitter on the sea . . ."

I gained fully three inches with the next tug.

" I've always said," remarked John chattily, " that you won't beat the West Coast sunsets anywhere. Not for richness and variety, anyway."

Nothing happened at the next tug. I was beginning to feel like an obscure Roman slave, who, trying to save what few possessions he has from a devastating fire, finds the sound of fiddling irksome.

" Really, Alastair," said John, " you ought to look. It's wonderful. You'll never see anything like it again."

I think I contrived to speak calmly, but I would not swear to it.

" John," I said. " One word more out of you, and you certainly will never see anything like it again. One more syllable about sunsets, and I shall strangle you, slowly, when I get down. If I get down. Which I doubt. Do you follow me ? "

"You needn't be rude about it," said John.

Sandy waited until I had passed the worst of it, and then pointed out, as diffidently as possible, that if that were the sunset, and we were facing it, then we had just ascended and descended the west and difficult side of the Inaccessible Pinnacle.

"Which," he added, "is no place for little boys." We were all a little thoughtful after that.

III

Curiously enough, our most serious mistake did not occur until the end of the holiday, when we had survived the worst of our apprenticeship and were learning sense at last. We had reached the stage when we could pass with freedom among the rock-peaks and feel at home on a precipice ; but we had still to learn the most important lesson in climbing, which is that the worst accidents happen at the easiest places. It is popularly held that mountaineers find themselves on occasion in vertical cul-de-sacs from which there is no escape, and so perish ; or that a slip is made on a particularly severe passage, with the same result. Fact is not so melodramatic.   The fatal accidents which have come about in either of these ways in Scotland could be counted on the fingers of one hand.

The reason is obvious to any one who has climbed. In such places the danger is self-evident ; and the climber, who is as fond of living as the next man, takes good care that he does not fall. He surmounts the difficulty, reaches easier ground, takes off the rope, puts his hands in his pockets, trips over his own feet, and breaks his neck. It is the old, old story of the racing motorist who died by stepping on a banana skin ; and it causes most mountaineering accidents. Height in itself is not necessarily a difficulty, but it is always a danger ; and climbers who allow themselves to become contemptuous of height sometimes forget this. Because, technically speaking, the ground is easy, they cease to take precautions. But the big drop is still there.

We learned this lesson late in the holiday. We went to Coir' a' Ghrunnda, another of the immense basins carved by the old glaciers from the flanks of the Cuillin. High up in the corrie nothing whatever grew. As the heather thinned and gave way to gabbro, we saw ahead of us a solid rampart of slabs, ground smooth by ice, stretching almost unbroken from side to side of the corrie like the concrete face of a dam. There is, I believe, a way through high up on the left ; but the only way we could find was a thin chimney in the centre of the rampart down which poured a waterfall. It was not too difficult, and soon we pulled ourselves out into an upper corrie, a bare bowl of rock more than half a mile across, naked as a pudding-basin, peppered with boulders, and decorated on its floor by one small loch. Around us were strange peaks with stranger names—Sgurr Sgumain, Sgurr Alasdair, Sgurr Dubh na Da Bheinn, Caisteal a' Garbh-choire, and Sgurr nan Eag—all high above us, though we ourselves were more than two thousand feet above the sea. One of the two eagles which haunted the southern Cuillin that year soared overhead, making height against the wind. It was a grim spot.

We wasted time there, then chose an easy scramble

to the summit of Sgurr Sgumain and spent the afternoon on the skyline, moving over a succession of tops until Coir' a' Ghrunnda lay behind us and Coire Lagan had taken its place. By this time we were tired. We were on the rim of another and even greater bowl, a rim which was much serrated and bounded by steep cliffs both inside and out. At length —it was about six o'clock at night, and we were still more tired and in a fitting frame of mind to make mistakes—we found ourselves at the bottom of a deep notch in the skyline, faced with an impossibly overhanging cliff well over a hundred feet high. There was only one thing we could do : we had to leave the crest, and take to the inside wall of the bowl, hoping that after we had traversed for a short distance we should be able to break back on to the skyline once more.

There was nothing in the least difficult about this move. The peak we were on was called Sgurr Mhic Coinnich, and the wall of Sgurr Mhic Coinnich which we proposed to traverse is amply supplied with wide ledges, one of which leads up to the skyline almost immediately. This, unfortunately, was not the ledge we chose ; and soon we found ourselves travelling parallel with the skyline, but with no prospect of climbing back on to it. We were not unduly worried. We were still heading in the right direction, and the ledge we were on was wide and easy. Any one could have walked along it with his hands in his pockets provided he kept his eyes open. But there were other things than the ledge to attract one's eyes. The mist had been low all day, forming a flat, grey ceiling which only just cleared the peaks and cut out all sight of the sun. Now the sun was almost setting, and had dropped low enough to shine in under the edge of the ceiling, so that to the west the grey of mist and wet rock opened out into the beginnings of a magnificent sunset. I remember thinking that John who had stayed below that day would be enjoying it. It was just after that that the first accident happened.

We were unroped, and William and Sandy were ahead of me. They had seen, and jumped over, an insecure block which formed part of the ledge's level floor, and passed from my sight round a corner. I was watching the sunset. I rested my hand casually on a hold, and stepped on to the block. After a confused instant when the earth turned over, I found myself where I had been before, only six feet of the ledge had disappeared and I was hanging by one hand. There was complete silence for what seemed to me like minutes. Then the block burst like a bomb three hundred feet below. I found another handhold, and felt sick.

There was silence again. William, out of sight round the corner, spoke in a quiet and very frightened voice.

"Are you all right, Alastair?" he said. He knew what must have happened, and was almost certain that I was no longer there.

"Anything but," I said, and giggled because it was such a silly answer. My stomach felt as if it did not belong to me. William came round the corner and hauled me to safety.

I lit a cigarette rather shakily while we considered ways and means. One thing was certain; I was not going any farther. There was an easy way down from the notch in the skyline, and I was going back to look

for it.   William thought this over and decided to come
with me.   He, too, he said, was not feeling particularly
cheerful.   The only difficulty was Sandy, who, well
ahead as usual, did not want to come back from what
looked like a perfectly simple way home ; and no
amount of long-distance arguing would move him from
this decision.   We did not know then that he had
crossed a rather nasty section of the ledge, and was
unwilling to recross it.   So it was agreed.   Sandy
should continue along the ledge, and we should descend
by a series of easy scree-shoots below the notch.

Slithering down scree is not nearly so alarming
as it looks or sounds, and Skye scree is the best in
the country.   Most of it is composed of millions of
stones about the size of a fist or a little bigger, and
the whole mass appears to move as you career
downwards, making a heartening clatter.   Scree,
commonly thought to be dangerous, is absolutely
safe.   High speeds are possible on it.   To run on it is
not unlike ski-ing without skis, and is undoubtedly
the easiest and quickest way of descending a rock
peak.   So William and I were beginning to feel a
little better by the time we were half-way down the
wall of Coire Lagan ; but we had been completely
cut off from sounds of Sandy's progress by the noise
of the stones we dislodged.   Half-way down we
stopped, and shouted to him.   There was no reply.
We thought this a little odd ; but, concluding that he
must be behind an angle of rock which prevented his
hearing us, moved on again and tried once more at the
bottom.   Still there was no reply.   Though we shouted
for ten minutes, we heard nothing but echoes.   William
looked at me with a queer expression on his face.

We felt very small and helpless, standing there below the cliffs of Mhic Coinnich. A thin drizzle of rain was falling ; and we were cold, and wet, and scared, and did not know which way to turn, for Sandy could have been almost anywhere on half a mile of cliff. We hung about, undecided, for another five minutes, shouting occasionally, and straining into the silence for some sound of a voice or a falling stone which would mean life where no life seemed to be. By this time we were very frightened indeed. We had almost given up hope when we heard a faint call from the far end of the cliff. It was Sandy, and he was shouting for help. The edge was taken off our worry by the sweat and clatter of our scramble up the cliff towards him.

We were almost indignant when we found him, for we could see that he was on a wide ledge, in no apparent danger, and with two simple routes from which to choose if he wanted to reach the easy ground thirty feet below on which we stood. We shouted that there was no difficulty, upon which he stood up, swayed once, and collapsed. I looked at William. He was all eyes and no face, like a child caught stealing. With one accord we clambered upwards.

Sandy was in quite a considerable mess. His face was yellow, his chin was split open, and there was a good deal of blood about. He had been unconscious for about twenty minutes. It seemed that after he had left us he had followed the ledge until his way was barred by a gap which had no handholds of any kind except one small knob high on the wall near the far side. It was difficult—far too difficult—but his judgment by this time was not all it might have been,

for Sandy, when scared, does not go slower as ordinary
mortals do, but goes faster. He had been scared and
going progressively faster almost since we had left him ;
and when he reached the gap he had taken one look at
the knob and jumped for it, a thing no climber in his
senses would have dreamed of doing. And the knob, as
he discovered when his fingers no more than touched
and slid off it, was no hold at all. It was all very
unfortunate. Events, from that point on, began to
happen at the speed of thirty-two feet per second per
second.

There was a wide chimney below, with two blocks
jammed between its walls ; and the first of these
blocks he struck with his knees in such a way that he
pitched outwards, head first, and struck the second
block a glancing blow with his chest as he shot past.
After that, he carried on for another twelve feet or so,
touching nothing, and landed on his hands. All told
he must have fallen twenty feet, most of them head
first, " with," as he said later, " my eyes open, so that
I could see what was coming to me. I didn't have time
to be frightened ; and the only feeling I had was one of
regret that it should happen this way. It seemed a pity,
but not awfully important."

We propped him up on the ledge, and made an
inventory. Two sprained wrists. Item, two sprained
elbows. Item, one bruised chest. Item, two bruised
knees. Item, one split chin. Item, shock. But by a
miracle, no bones were broken ; and he said he thought
he could walk. We tied him on the rope and lowered
him over the edge. After that our real troubles began.

Scree-running, as has been pointed out, is an
excellent method for descending mountains ; but

"running" is the operative word, and Sandy could not walk unassisted. The art of scree-running lies in travelling as fast as, or faster than, the little avalanche of stones upon which the climber is riding. If he should travel less quickly than the avalanche, the ground slips away from under his feet, which is precisely what happened that night, and thoroughly unpleasant it was. Sandy had one damaged arm round each of our necks, so that we were competing in a slipping, stumbling four-legged race with the scree which was steep and loose and leading by a canter all the way. We fell repeatedly. Every now and then Sandy was sick.

It was while this was happening that the sunset staged a blatant piece of symbolism. The rock of the Cuillin possesses to a remarkable degree the chameleon-like ability to suit its colour to its surroundings, taking its cue from the sun, so that on dull days the rock, naturally grey-brown, appears to be black, whereas at a clear dawn it may be green or blue. When the rock is wet, this effect is heightened. It was wet that night. The sunset, by now on the horizon and pouring in unobstructed under the misty ceiling, was blood-red. The result was pure Grand Guignol. The miles of cliffs which enclosed us seemed to be streaming blood. I felt about one inch high.

Sandy, by now on almost level heather, and a little recovered, looked at it and shook his head.

"Now that," he said, "is what I call really bad taste."

IV

That was the end of the holiday, and, for three of us, almost the end of climbing. Sandy went back to London with most of Glenbrittle's supply of sticking-plaster disposed about his person; and as London, lacking height, has only two dimensions, his climbing was over for a year. The other two, though they lived near the hills, were involved in study and could not spare the time to visit them. I had to find other companions.

I found them week-end by week-end in strange places, separated by many miles of country and many hours of work in the city. The construction of this book, therefore, must change. Continuous narrative is impossible, because for those who climb or walk each week-end is complete in itself. The story of the open air in Scotland, whoever should tell it, is not a novel or a biography : it is a collection of short stories, each with its own characters.

Before I saw Skye again I was to learn very little about mountains, but a great deal about people.

CHAPTER FOUR

THE CAVE

ON many of the week-ends which followed I went to those Youth Hostels which lay within easy reach of Glasgow. I went because there I found a world whose existence I had not been brought up to expect, and because I liked the people who lived in it. It was a young world, governed by the young. I was twenty at the time, and most of the people I met were my own age ; people who, like myself, had only recently discovered that they could leave city, class, and the orthodoxy of their elders behind them at week-ends and create their own lives for a day and a half a week beyond the influence of these things

There had been walkers, and cyclists, and climbers before ; but not in these numbers. The great hiking craze of the early nineteen-thirties, which sent thousands, curiously clad, out into the country for the first time, was the beginning of it all as a mass movement. It was artificial, and died as these crazes do, but not before it had launched the Youth Hostel movement and established a solid body of young men and girls who took exercise because they enjoyed it, and not because they liked wearing funny trousers. Few of these people had any money to spare. Many of them cycled to their hostel, and most of the others patronized only those hostels which could be reached cheaply by bus or train. But there were also those who either could not afford transport and the shilling a night it cost to stay at a hostel, or did not choose to afford them.

They camped in summer, and in the winter slept as tramps do, in caves and barns. So at that time there was a great coming and going upon the roads on Saturdays and Sundays by as strangely assorted a mass of people as were ever moved by the same urge to do the same things at the same time. And so it is to this day.

These were the people I came to know ; and, knowing them, found they had a caste system which was based, not upon rank, but upon performance. There were the cyclists, the hikers, the climbers, each of them an almost separate society living in amity with the other groups, but wrapped up in its own affairs. Thus, although no test of accent or social class would reveal any division in a hostel common room, it would be found that cyclists for the most part talked with cyclists, and hikers with hikers. In the same way, there were friendly distinctions within each of the groups. Among the cyclists were the tourers, the long-distance men, the speed men. Among the climbers were the members of the old-established clubs, most of them reasonably well-to-do ; and the members of the new clubs, most of them anything but well-to-do ; and both of these could be still further sub-divided into mountaineers and hill-walkers. The hikers alone achieved anything like a unity, and that only through their variety : they came from every level of society, and their exploits defied classification. And there were the professional people of the roads, the haakers, the minks, and the flatties, who had never seen the inside of a youth hostel and had no desire for the experience. But they come later in the story. At first I knew only the hostels. Then I visited the cave.

II

The lad with the clinker-nailed boots and the rope in his rucksack who told me how to find the cave made me promise to keep the secret ; and though crowds from the local youth hostel wander up to it every week-end now, I still do not feel inclined to set down in detail the little map he drew for me on a sheet torn from an old railway time-table. But this much I can say. I was to follow a track to a forester's cottage, pass through a gate which I was to be sure to close behind me for fear some beasts might stray, and there search for an old sheep fank. Behind it I should find a faint track leading up the hillside ; and if I followed the scratches on the rock it led to, I should find the cave and good company.

This was during the winter of 1933. I was only beginning to realise that one of the greatest charms of climbing, or walking, or cycling was the people one met on the road. I was still more concerned with the pure mechanics of climbing, and until then had dealt more with rock than with people. But the cave had sounded exciting, and I had nothing else to do that week-end. I had packed my rucksack and caught the Saturday afternoon bus north.

There was snow in the glen, so there were footprints to guide me ; but when the path petered out on to slabs of rock the way was more difficult to follow, for it was dusk, and the rock was clear of snow. Centuries before, a cliff had given up the struggle against rain and frost, and had collapsed, splitting into blocks bigger than houses as it fell, and forming a maze which had depth as well as length and breadth, like coals in an

unlit fire. The biggest block was a pyramid high as a
tenement, and it came to rest with its base straddling
two smaller blocks, so that a space was left underneath.
The rubbish of ages filled in the sides, and to-day the
only entrances to the space below the pyramid are two
small holes which appear to lead directly to the bowels
of the earth. The only other opening is a small hole
in the roof, blackened by the smoke of fires which have
been lit below it since the days, hundreds of years ago,
when there was a drove-road through the glen.

I must have climbed past the main entrance, for
the first sign of life I found was a hole in the ground
from which smoke was curling. It seemed I was
too high, so I dropped thirty feet and tried again.
This time I smelled kippers, and followed my nose.
It led to a narrow cleft, five feet high, framing a patch
of utter darkness redolent of wood smoke and cooking,
but apparently bottomless. It was not a good place
to tackle without a torch.

" Oi ! " I shouted.

" You've been rakin' aboot oot there for hauf an
hoor," remarked a calm voice from the inner darkness.
" Whit aboot comin' in for a change ? The kippers
is jist aboot ready."

I slid downwards and arrived suddenly and
decisively on the floor of the cave. It was a big place
—about forty feet square, with a roof fifteen feet
high, jagged walls and a sloping earth floor scattered
with boulders—and there were three young men squatting
round a fire, frying kippers and dangling on a wire
over the flames a large black pudding. A layer of
smoke clung to the roof as ground-mist clings to a
hollow on an autumn evening. It fretted evenly back

and forth, swirling suddenly as a gust of wind blew back
down the chimney, and then continuing its slow search
for the outer world. The air was clear at ground level,
and the fire burned well. The cave looked almost
cosy.

The lad who had spoken before nodded in much
the same way as men nod to a late arrival in a coffee
room, and said : " Kippers or black puddin', mate ?
Or a wee tate o' both ? " So I sat down and had both,
and then cast about for my frying pan so that I could
add my own food to the meal.

" My name's Andy," said the cook ; " what's
yours ? And that's Callum, and that's George. Are
these sausages ye have there ? "

George was a shy youth with a long, solemn face
and big hands. He wore a blue sailor's jersey and
aged climbing breeches, much patched about the
knees and seat ; and he held out his frying-pan to me
when he saw me begin to search for my own.

" Here, mate," he said. " Nae sense in dirtyin'
two."

He sat watching me in silence while the other
two talked. It was surprisingly difficult to realise
that we had only just met, and that I had not sat before
with my back against this concave boulder and my feet
half into the red embers of the fire, listening to stories.
" My name's Andy. What's yours ? " No lengthy
explanations, no fuss. It was pleasant to be taken at
one's face value like that. Andy talked as if he had
known me for years.

He was small and wiry, with a twinkle in his eye
and a friendly grin which revealed that one of his front
teeth was missing, a relic, he said, of the day when the

snow was down on the Campsie Fells and he had attempted, with complete lack of success but with spectacular results, to climb Coffin Gully, using as an ice-axe a ninepenny trenching tool. He delighted in telling stories against himself. At one point in all of them he would say: " And there was me . . ." and would follow with a description of some appalling predicament he had landed in through bad luck or his own fecklessness; but his misfortunes were told without bitterness, as enormous jokes; and when the climax came with a fall down a mountainside or a night spent, soaked and freezing, under a hedge, he always laughed louder than his audience at the rich humour of it all.

" Jings ! " he would say, " it was an awfu' night. We was daein' oor best to sleep in a railway bothy we called the Howff of the Thousand Draughts, and us soakin' and chitterin' wi' the cauld. Ye see, the bothy was made wi' auld railway sleepers, and the man that made it didna fill up thon holes they stick the rails on tae. And there was me, fair blue, stickin' lumps o' the *Glasgow Herald* in them to try for to keep the draught oot."

At which the entire company, and Andy louder than any one, would howl with laughter.

Callum was a massive creature with a chuckle which rumbled deep down inside him under many thicknesses of sweaters. His boots, smothered in mountaineering nails, were enormous. He was content to act as claque to Andy's story-telling; but he chuckled wholeheartedly, and seemed more at ease than the silent George, who sat sombrely beyond the fire, saying nothing.

The cave, I gathered, was club-room and hotel for the Creag Dhu Mountaineering Club, some of whose members I had already met on the Cobbler. Most of them came from Clydebank, at that time a place of empty shipyards and crowded street corners, a smoky arm of Glasgow where nothing ever happened except the regular visit to the " Burroo " and an odd drink to celebrate the coming up of that insult to the law of averages, the three-cross double.

Some of the cave-dwellers were unemployed, some not ; but the urge which took them to the hills each week-end had been born in unemployment and the determination of young men not to waste all their lives idle in the reek of Clydeside while there were mountains and glens, neglected for generations, on their own doorsteps. Once born, the idea reproduced itself in hundreds of minds. These lads, bred in Yoker and the dreich stretch of Dumbarton Road, had found themselves at home in the hills, and treasured their cave as a child will treasure his hidey-hole in the woods where he can sit with a wooden sword and be a brigand chief. Only there was this difference. They lived in the cave because they could afford to live nowhere else ; and they did not play at being mountaineers, but were mountaineers, some of them among the most skilful and hardy I have met.

Transport, of course, was their problem, for bus and railway fares cost money, and there is very little which is worth climbing within reach of a Glasgow man who has not at least five shillings to spend. This was the fact which gave the cave its characteristic bustle, for only people who travel by trains or buses arrive at their destination at stated times. The cavemen travelled on their thumbs. Long before the movies spread details of the transatlantic technique of hitch-hiking, the Clydebank crew had evolved one of their own—a pathetic limp, an inordinately heavy rucksack, and a thumb waved in front of on-coming traffic in the direction in which they wished to travel. It seldom failed. Somehow or other, on lorries, in private cars, or (the miracle is talked of yet) in a police patrol car, they contrived to find their way north before dawn to bed down among the boulders on the floor of the cave beside their friends, who had been dropping through the door in twos and threes since the previous afternoon.

Some one was always arriving. For instance, I had just dealt with the black pudding, and was beginning to wonder who was going to clean the kipper pan, and with what, when a large lad, red-haired and grinning broadly, fell through the doorway and solved the pan problem by adding sausages to what had gone before. He announced in a matter-of-fact tone that Jackie and he had tossed for one vacant seat in a car ten miles back, and that Jackie had lost. He apparently had such faith in Jackie's powers of persuasion that he expected him to arrive at any minute. Which he did. Quarter of an hour later he jumped down into the cave and added liver to the sorely-tried frying pan and capped the lot with two eggs poured from a screw-topped jar.

George still kept to his corner. He seemed to be a stranger; and, though the crowd was willing to accept him, he held back.

By ten o'clock at night a dozen people had, literally, dropped in. Then Jolly (he was the long man with the sausages) produced a mouth organ, wiped it solemnly on the hem of his jersey, and began to play softly while one of the later arrivals burrowed in his rucksack and found a jews' harp.

Everybody sang. And they did not sing jazz, which is good to dance to and may even be whistled, but is the curse of all singing and an affront to any one who has heard good songs sung loudly in company. The songs that the Creag Dhu sang were the early hill-billies and cowboy songs (composed by men not unlike themselves) ; and there they showed taste, for, though they probably did not know that the difference existed, they instinctively avoided the modern Tin-Pan Alley versions of the old tunes and confined themselves to those from which the new saccharine versions have sprung—songs with twenty verses apiece about cowboys who want to be buried out on the lone prairee ; and engine drivers, generally called Casey Jones, who are killed, round about verse eighteen, in train smashes. "Frankie and Johnnie" was one, of course, and "The Wreck of the Ninety-Nine." Some one sang "The Engineer" as a solo ; and there was one mournful ditty called "The Dying Mountaineer."

There were others, too, born on this side of the Atlantic and north of the Border—the Bothy Ballads, out of Buchan and the Mearns. They are old, and may not be sung in polite company ; but they are grand songs, and it is sad that they should be dying. But in the cave they were preserved ; and you could roar at the pitch of your voice and think what a rowdy, satisfactory art the world lost when the first crooner saw the first microphone and the Students' Songbook vanished from the land.

Clydebank and the cave were far apart that night. The rock walls curved, smoke-blackened, to a ceiling out of sight in the darkness overhead. The only light came from the fire, and two candles capping a boulder on the floor. Round the fire and beside the candles were the Creag Dhu, in the darkness only fragments of them and their trappings visible—legs swathed in puttees, coarse flannel shirts open at the neck, hefty climbing-boots, an odd coil of alpine rope, an ice-axe or two (it was January, and the hills were in grand condition), and, jutting into the light, strong, chunky faces—a careless, shouting crew. Jolly blew on his mouth organ and tried to make himself heard above the din. The man with the jews' harp was inspired. Somewhere in the darkness was a fine tenor.

As the shouting grew, others arrived. We had eighteen in residence in the end, and the last man (he arrived after midnight) sang a solo with a sausage poised half-way to his mouth. Then they told stories. They were all keen climbers, and the tales jumped from Skye to the Cairngorms, from Ben Nevis to Arrochar, and then back north to Glencoe. They seemed to have been in every conceivable variety of scrape on every conceivable variety of mountain, and the bigger the scrape (there were many there of Andy's philosophy) the louder the laughter. They started with an all-night crossing of Ben Lomond, when the snow was waist-deep, and they blessed the sheep which had ploughed tunnels a man could follow until he came on the sheep dead at the end of them ; and then some one said, " D'you mind the time when . . ." and they were off to the ludicrous story of the bothy that had no door (they thought it funny, but it had nearly cost one of them his life), and the tale of the man who camped for a fortnight under three sheets of corrugated iron and survived storms which washed out every camper in the glen.

A little after one in the morning they began to turn in. They rolled themselves in blankets, and fell asleep round the fire, with boots protruding from one end of each cocoon and a balaclava helmet from the other, laid skilfully here and there between the boulders on the uneven floor. They slept almost immediately.

Before I spread out my sleeping-bag and lay down beside George, I went outside to see the moon slip down behind the mountains across the glen. The night was clear and hard, and frost sparkled on the rim of the cave door. The glen was spread out below, glittering in the fast disappearing moonlight, for the snow was down, and frozen. And, as I stood there with the silence in front and the sound of deep breathing behind, and the moon sliding finally behind the mountains, I knew the satisfaction of being a brigand with a wooden sword, and being independent of any mechanical thing.

III

It must have been three o'clock when I woke, conscious that something had disturbed me. George heard it too, for I felt him stiffen.

"This is the place," said a voice which did not sound too happy.

The cave was in darkness, for the fire was dead; but a beam from an electric torch cut through it and went crawling crab-wise over the bodies on the floor.

Some of them stirred, and mumbled into sleep again. I could not tell how many men were standing behind the torch at the door.

"Would you know him if you saw him?" asked the first voice.

"Ay. Passed him on the road this afternoon."

The light flickered across Andy's face and he woke and sat up.

"Hey, you. What's your name?" said the voice.

"Eh?"

"What's your name?"

"Och, awa' tae blazes!"

"Less of that. This is the police, and I'm asking your name."

Andrew was clearly sceptical. "Ay. You're the polis," he said, lying down again and settling into a comfortable position, "and I'm Ramsay MacDonald. Awa' and let a fella get some sleep." Suddenly he was smitten by doubt, and shot up again. "Here, you're no' really the polis, are ye? Oh, jings!"

He gave his name and address. So did I, when my turn came, to an invisible figure standing behind a torch which dazzled me. I turned out my kit, too, as we all had to do, and watched the torch rake it as if (and it seemed credible to me that it should, so unreal was the whole performance) the policeman behind it expected to find diamond necklaces among my old jerseys. The torch travelled on to a George grown unexpectedly bold. He gave his name without being asked, and grinned unabashed as the policeman's voice dropped and became even more gruff.

"It's you we want," said the policeman. "You'd better pack."

"I'll come," said George, "but you're daft. I didnae dae it."

"Maybe you're right," said the policeman peaceably, "but you'd better come along just the same."

"O.K.," said George, and that was that, without fuss or unpleasantness. Within five minutes we were left to our cave, and what remained of the night. The last we heard of George was as he helped and encouraged one of the policemen across the slippery rocks beyond the door.

"Look. Pit your left foot there," he said. "No. Not there. *There*. Oh, man, you'll nivver get doon at this rate."

The scraping of boots faded in the distance. There was silence.

"Look here," said Andy at last. "Whit's a' this aboot? Eh? Whit's the fella supposed to have done?"

No one replied.

"Well," said Andy, "does any one ken who he is?"

Apparently no one did, though one lad thought he might have seen him down Partick way at a meeting.

"Ah, well," said Andy, yawning, "he looked a dacent-like spud tae me, onyway. I hope he gets awa' wi' it."

We grunted, "Hear, hear," and slept.

IV

I never met George again, for he was not a member of the Creag Dhu—and did not, I think, climb at all;

but I did not like to leave a story hanging in mid-air. And, after all, George had lent me his frying-pan. I spent most of Monday morning in trying to find out what had happened to him, and found it a difficult job. The local police denied all knowledge of the affair and suggested, in the politest manner possible, that I was either romancing or suffering from delusions ; but they added, as an afterthought, that it was just possible the county police might have made the arrest.

The headquarters of the county police was a house of many mansions ; and to the accompaniment of " Thrrree minutes, six minutes, nine minutes " by the girl on the telephone exchange I was shunted from department to department until I reached an extremely Highland sergeant who admitted that something of the sort might have happened. He would go and find out.

" Yess," he said when he returned to the telephone five minutes later, " a man answering to your description wass brought in early on Sunday morning. Bút he wass not exactly what you would call arrested. He wass released a few hours later."

" Not exactly what I would call arrested ? " I said. " But confound it, man, I was there. I saw it happen."

The sergeant was polite, but firm. " No, no," he said, " he wass not arrested. Not at aall. He wass chust apprehended for investigation. That wass aall. Chust apprehended for investigation. Good morning to you, sir."

So now you know all about it.

CHAPTER FIVE

CHOOCHTER

THANKS to the cave, I came much in contact during the months which followed with the members of that small but persevering class known as the hitch-hikers. Their chief interest, in some cases approaching the proportions of a religion, was climbing ; and hitch-hiking, or the art of tapping lifts, was their method of bringing good mountains within reach of the city.

There are those who take an uncharitable view of this activity, claiming that the man who begs for lifts is no better than the man who begs for pennies, but I prefer to think of the hitch-hiker as the twentieth century troubadour. Once the troubadour was welcome at any castle, for he earned his keep by song, and song was thought good value for the money. So it is with hitch-hiking in its higher forms, as it is practised on the Loch Lomond road to-day. Words, and not song, are the hitch-hiker's capital. I have met them silent ; but as a class they can give the Irish points in dialectic, and they turn a story well. Driving is a boring task. Many a good tale has been told, and many a dull journey enlivened between the Arrochar road-end and Anniesland Cross.

Some of the tales smack of the epic, and not in construction alone, for some hitch-hiking feats verge upon the fabulous. For years the record was held by a lad who left Glasgow with half a crown in his pocket and intent to camp in Skye, and tapped a lift on the outskirts of the city which took him to Sligachan Inn, two hundred miles away and not two hundred yards from the spot where he had intended camping; but recently this feat has dwindled to insignificance as the brotherhood has realised the full possibilities of the thumb as a mode of transport. In 1936 one Glasgow lad travelled to Paris for three shillings, tapping lifts on both sides of the Channel and making a charming smile bridge the gap created by his ignorance of the French language. His only extra was his cross-Channel fare. And in 1937 two of the Creag Dhu, finding themselves idle and with time hanging heavily on their hands, tapped lifts to Switzerland and back. The tale goes, too, that they even hitch-hiked up the Matterhorn behind a guided party.

But these are examples of the art in its pure state, the simple situation of one or more friendly hitch-hikers meeting one car. Let competition creep in, and the whole situation is altered. Given two or more hard-bitten and hostile hitch-hikers infesting the same stretch of road, the game becomes more than a straightforward gamble on empty seats and sympathetic drivers. It becomes a battle of wits, based on the good Biblical truth that the last shall be first and the first shall be last. It must be so, for the one immutable rule in competitive hitch-hiking is that the last man gets the first lift : on any road, the man who lags farthest behind is the first to be overtaken by passing traffic, and therefore has the advantage of any more energetic souls who may have walked on ahead. Consequently, fantastic battles have been waged by

rival hitch-hikers who have tried to walk fast enough
to reach their destination in the event of no lifts being
obtainable, and slow enough to remain last all the
time.

The best story I have heard about this peculiar
mode of travelling was told to me one November night
at Arrochar by a gentleman rejoicing in the name of
Choochter. What far-fetched process of corruption
and illusion created this nickname I do not know ;
but Choochter he was, and I never knew him by any
other name. He was tall and thin, with a slight stoop.
A lock of hair hung down almost over one eye, and his
climbing jacket and breeches were patched after the
homely manner of all climbing jackets and breeches.
His accent was such that any one born beyond the
bounds of Glasgow would have found much in
his conversation that was obscure. He was as
companionable a lad as one would care to meet ; and
I first fell in with him while he was buying half a pound
of sausages in the butcher's shop at Arrochar. He
had travelled up from Glasgow free, of course. I
bought what I wanted ; and it was while we walked
together down the road to the Youth Hostel that he
told me the story of himself, Wullie, Ginger, and Wee
Jock.

It seemed that Choochter and Ginger had been
on the point of leaving the Vale of Leven for a few
days' climbing in Glencoe, sixty miles away, when
they were smitten by a desire to eat chips ; and, as
all the world knows, there is a shop just before the start
of the Loch Lomond road, which has something of a
reputation for chips. There they had gone, and there
had met the opposition—Wullie and Wee Jock.

" In his kilt," Choochter added, as if that made it much worse.

" Wullie was just gettin' tore into a poke o' chips," said Choochter, " so we pretended we was goin' on ahead. O' course, we hid in ahint the first dyke we came to ; and in a wee while, by goes Wullie and Wee Jock, in his kilt, stuffin' themselves wi' chips. We waits anither two-three minutes just for to gi'e them a start, and then sets aff, slow-like."

For an hour they had walked on, leaving the houses behind them and dropping down to the rolling country which falls to the south end of Loch Lomond, confidently expecting first rights on any car which should pass. But as they reached the loch Choochter glanced behind him, stopped, and swore. It was, he saw, going to be a hard night. The fight was on. Diamond was about to cut diamond. For Wee Jock (in his kilt) was a hundred yards behind, emerging cautiously, like a mouse from the wainscoat, from behind a hedge. Choochter sighed, and cast about for cover.

The sides were fairly matched ; and, an aptitude for guile being strongly developed in all concerned and the means of their journey appealing more to them than its end, compromise at this stage did not occur to them. From that point on, all thoughts of progress seem to have been abandoned, and the journey resolved itself into long waits behind walls and trees, grubbings about in bushes, occupations of darkened barns, an elaborate game of chess in which the only popular move was the knight's. Leap-frogging ahead and aside, a fresh ambush was prepared at almost every bend in the road. Tactics of a high order were employed. At one stage both parties were even travelling backwards.

The night grew darker, and traffic thinner. Despite piteous thumbings, no car stopped ; and as eleven o'clock came and went their hopes dwindled. Even the chance of spending the night at Inverbeg Youth Hostel, a few miles ahead, had disappeared as time and energy were dissipated behind hedges.

" It was cuttin' wur ain throats, mister ; it was cuttin' wur ain throats," said Choochter solemnly.

Stalemate was reached shortly before midnight, when lack of traffic made further efforts useless. Choochter and Ginger gave up for the night somewhere near Luss, where they found a bell-tent left unoccupied at the side of the loch by some trusting soul, and crawled inside, working on the assumption that, as the tent was completely empty, no one would be likely to claim it at that hour of the night.

" We woke early . . six o'clock," said Choochter. " We'd nae blankets, and I was sleepin' in a *Glasgow Herald* and a sheet o' broon paper. Ginger woke first. He was in an *Express*, but the pages is far ower wee. He wallapped me in the ribs and pointed oot' o' the tent.

" ' Look at thon ! ' " he says, fair wild.

" I looks ; and there lyin' on the verandy o' a hoose-boat at the loch-side, was Wullie and Wee Jock, in his kilt."

A nice question of tactics was involved. Wee Jock, having, as has been noted, a kilt as well as a *Glasgow Herald* to keep him warm, was still sound asleep and might be expected to remain so for at least an hour, leaving the road clear for Choochter and Ginger. But traffic was scarce at that hour of the morning : there are few milk-producing farms north of Luss, and no milk-lorries run to and from the city. The most they could hope for was a stray carrier's van, and even that hope was slender. Besides, if they should fail to tap a lift before Wee Jock awoke, they would leave him with first chance of all lifts for the rest of the day. They decided to lie in hiding until the other two should wake and move on.

The three hours which followed were, according to Choochter, desperate. During two of them, Wullie and Wee Jock slept, the dew of the morning wet on their raincoats, while the sun came up behind Ben Lomond and the island-shadows shortened on the Luss Narrows. The morning mist died in the treetops. And still they slept. It was a bright, clear morning, and bitterly cold for those who had little but the daily press to shield them from the chill shadows of the tent. Most galling sight of all was breakfast on the houseboat, which started at eight-thirty. Wee Jock produced a folding stove from his rucksack, and Wullie cooked slowly and deliberately, an operation which nearly broke Choochter's heart, for, as he so delicately put it, he and Ginger had " nae chuck " and were exceedingly hungry. But in the end they packed and moved off, leaving the others lying on their empty stomachs, contemplating nature.

" We gi'ed them hauf an hoor's start this time, and aff we went. Hauf an hoor. Jings, man, we thought we had them this time, though the wait near kilt us wi' hunger and the cauld. But . . . ach . . . we hudni' gone more nor a mile affore I looks back ; and there, jookin' in ahint the last corner, was Wee Jock, in his kilt. Man, it was chronic."

From nine until noon the running fight continued, first one side gaining the rear, then the other, for the Loch Lomond road is thickly wooded, with cover for an ambushing army. They hid in drains and ditches; they lolled by the lochside in the hope that the others were drawing out of reach and competition; they tossed for ha'pennies in the woods until the others should pass. But when both parties met behind the same hedge, each thinking the other was in the rear, a peace conference was obviously called for. In three hours they had covered only two miles.

They tossed for first lift. Ginger and Choochter won. All four walked on together for an hour until the first car responded to signals, and Wullie and Wee Jock were left in sole possession of the road. It was a good lift, and took Choochter and Ginger over Glen Falloch and beyond to Crianlarich and Tyndrum, where their driver branched off for Oban. They set out to walk the rest.

I should like to be able to record that five minutes later Wullie and Wee Jock drove by in a Rolls-Royce and were taken all the way to Glencoe; but well-turned plots happen seldom in real life. The truth of the matter was that the two stragglers were landed at the Tyndrum branch a few minutes later, and all four plodded on again together. After five miles (an unprecedented distance for a hitch-hiker to walk, according to Choochter) an aged but empty car stopped beside them, and its driver waved them towards him. He was an apologetic creature.

" I'm sorry to trouble you," he began, " but I'm going to Glencoe and want to find a certain hotel there.

Kingshouse Inn, it's called. I . . . I wonder if you could tell me where it is ? "

Choochter looked at the car. At a pinch it would carry them all. He smiled his most charming smile.

" It's a kinda difficult road to describe," he began, " but it wouldn't be takin' me and ma pals far oot o' oor way to show ye. We weren't really thinkin' o' goin' to Glencoe, ye ken, but . . ."

II

Shortly after this I was in Glencoe, heading south in a car with some friends, when Jake hailed us from the roadside. If we had been gifted with second sight, we should have driven on ; but we stopped, and that was the beginning of the trouble. Jake was small and stocky, and had a wide grin. His jacket and breeches were ragged, his puttees half off his legs, and his rucksack decorated with a climbing rope excessively large. He smiled a brazen smile and said he would like a lift to Glasgow, quite unconcerned by the fact that we did not know him from Adam.

He got his lift ; and it happened that on the way home I bewailed the fact that I could not raise a car for the following week-end, when I wanted to climb Ben Nevis. Jake, it appeared, also wanted to climb Ben Nevis, for it was under snow and in fine condition ; but he was puzzled to know why I considered a car necessary. I pointed out that Ben Nevis was more than a hundred miles from Glasgow by road, and that a car was the only feasible method of reaching it. Jake disagreed. It seemed he knew a lorry driver.

So the first act of the tragedy opened on the lorry,

a vehicle without grace or, it seemed, springs, Most of the action, lasting seven hours and played in total darkness, took place in a swaying oblong slot where we lay jammed between the cargo and the back of the lorry. On one side was the backboard, a heavy wooden wall designed to prevent goods falling backwards on to the road, and inscribed in gold letters on its outer face with the owner's name and occupation. The other side of our world was the cargo, which failed by a bare three feet to reach the back-board, and towered eight feet above us. It was a solid rampart of tea-chests. And the two ends opened directly on to the road.

There were, however, two other features worthy of note—the ceiling and the floor. The first of these was simply a tarpaulin laced tightly over the gap where the sky should have been ; but the second was of a more complicated character. We were not lying on the lorry floor proper. As the slot was almost exactly the width of a tea-chest, and as two had been left over when the rampart was completed, the lorryman had squeezed them in, and told us to lie on top of them. So far, so good. Space, however, still remained ; and to bring the rest of the floor up to our level the man had stuffed in three very dead sheep, skinned and neatly sewn up in sacks, with their heads sticking out and their throats cut.

In these surroundings, Jake and I tried to make ourselves comfortable. In order to get in at all, we had to lie nose to tail like sardines in a tin, so that my head dangled over the road, bumping against Jake's feet as it swung, while Jake's head was wedged in some unspeakable position among blood-stained sacking.

High above us, jammed between the tarpaulin and the top of the cargo, were our rucksacks.

We had our first taste of trouble before we were clear of Glasgow. Somewhere in Sauchiehall Street our rucksacks broke adrift from their moorings and fell down about our ears, without warning and with dire results. One of them fouled a sheep as it fell, and, judging by the muffled quality of the yells which followed, had buried Jake and the sheep in the same gory grave.

I started groping about in the darkness to discover what had happened to him, impeded both by the constricted nature of our bed and the fact that I was in a sleeping-bag, and not daring to unlace the tarpaulin. I had no desire to appear in Sauchiehall Street in a sleeping-bag, even at midnight ; and the one condition the lorry driver had imposed was that we kept under cover. It was not, I discovered, altogether easy to stand up in darkness on a swaying lorry, clad like a competitor in a sack-race, and to perform heavy manual labour while playing blind man's buff with three dead sheep and a squirming mountaineer. One rucksack had jammed across Jake's chest, and the other had forced a sheep over him and buried his head completely. It was a scene made for two-reel comedy ; but poor Jake, with a dead sheep's head nestling on his shoulder like a dyspeptic lawyer, was in no mood for slapstick. Nor, at the time, was I. It was a gory business.

After that we tried to settle down. I even managed to sleep after a fashion ; but Jake, although he had been to a dance on the previous night and had been up till all hours, did not sleep a wink. Rain began to drip through the tarpaulin. We rumbled northwards, heaving and creaking, and smelling most abominably of sheep.

When I woke, I was conscious that something violent had just happened, though what it had been I did not know. It was six in the morning, and light was seeping through the seams in the tarpaulin. The lorry had stopped, and there were voices outside. I felt as if I had gone over Niagara in a barrel, and was too sorry for myself to notice at first that we were listing badly ; but when it did occur to me that something was seriously wrong I climbed out of my bag and the lorry.

The morning was cold and grey ; and, as we were in Ballachulish, a spot famed for its slate quarries, the nearer landscape, too, was cold and grey. Above us lurched a hill of shattered slate, big as a slag-heap and buttressed with stone to prevent the whole mass avalanching over the square of grey houses at its base. It was a depressing sight. Still more depressing was the lorry, which had broken through a concealed drain in the centre of the square and foundered completely. The driver looked at us sourly.

" You'd better no' be here when the breakdown van arrives," he said. " The boss'll be on it. There's a bus for Fort William leaves here in half-an-hour."

So we reached Fort William ingloriously by bus ; and the first act closed when we pitched our tent beside Achentee Farm, which lies against the base of Ben Nevis.

III

Act Two was set upon the mountain. At the bottom was our tent. Two thousand feet up was the snowline ; and above it everything was white up to the cairn, 4406 feet above sea level. We had both felt seedy when we started ; and powder-snow, thigh-deep, followed by a gully with a quite uncalled for amount of ice in it, had kept us back and improved our condition not at all. So Act Two opened at precisely 7 p.m. on a night in January, at the top of Ben Nevis, in dense mist and a heavy snowstorm.

We were completely blind. Blindness, as it is commonly understood, is a state in which the victim is hampered by the fact that everything appears to be black ; but neither Jake nor I had realised until then that any colour may be substituted for black with the same result, provided only that the colour be consistent and have no light and shade.

I have never since known visibility so poor as it was that night. A little daylight was still being reflected by the snow, which was unbroken by any rocks ; but it was so diffused that there were no shadows and the snow was without texture. Mist merged so subtly with snow that they were the same shade of grey and it was impossible to tell where one stopped and the other began. By the evidence of our eyes we were walking in a cloud far above the earth, grey-blind in a world of no dimensions. Our eyes could not even tell us whether we were walking uphill or down, for the snow appeared to be no more substantial than the mist. We could only tell how the slope lay by the strain on our legs. If it were easy, then we were going down. If it were strenuous, we were climbing. And if we cut across a slope, we stumbled and fell continuously because we could not tell how much to bend the uphill knee. I have not walked under such conditions since, and do not hope to do so again. It had all the vivid unreality of those dreams in which one appears in a public place clad only in pyjamas.

Jake had an enormous floating-dial compass which would have been more at home on a ship than on his wrist ; but he and his compass led us clear of the mist by 8.30, at which stage we were plastered with snow and still had a shade more than 2000 feet to go. Then Jake said he would like a rest, and we sat down in the snow. A minute later, he was sound asleep.

The dance, the lorry, and the fact that he was not in training were beginning to tell. I shone our one torch on his face. He lay flat on a drift, his head cradled in the crook of an elbow, breathing gently as the snowflakes fell and melted on his face. I sat watching him, thinking in an almost impersonal way that I ought to be worried if only I had the heart or the energy to be worried, and wondering, quite placidly, how we were going to drag ourselves off the mountain. The torch did not disturb Jake. He slept on. In the end I kicked him to his feet, and we struggled downwards for another two or three hundred feet. By this time, Jake was being sick every five minutes or so, and was stumbling so badly that I called another halt. I think he would have dropped if we had not stopped. We lay down, and I timed him. He fell asleep inside twenty seconds.

The curious thing was that Jake, although fully aware of his condition, was not greatly concerned about it, and in the intervals between sickness and sickness kept on his face a sleepy travesty of his old grin.

" You keep kicking me, and I'll be O.K.," he said.

So every time he stopped, which was frequently, I punted him to his feet and the procession moved off again. Provided Jake did not collapse we were in no real danger, for we were on a path and knew the way down, and so long as the torch lasted it was just a matter of keeping on our feet until we reached the bottom. The only difficulty was that when we dropped below the snowline the going was much rougher, for stones and boulders, hitherto ironed out by the snow, had to be negotiated ; and the snowstorm had become a rainstorm with plenty of wind behind it. Not that that mattered to Jake. He could have slept anywhere by that time, and I am certain he was asleep on his feet for part of the way. Twice he fell, and on the second occasion hacked his shin so severely that for fifty yards he was almost lucid. Then the old beatific smile crept back to his face, and he dozed downwards once more.

We lost height slowly, and I kept my mind off things by dreaming of the exact grain and texture and flavour of the four chops I had in the tent, and of the meal we were going to have. Neither of us had eaten for eleven hours.

The final thousand feet were timeless, neither fast nor slow, for time was suspended and its place taken by a monotony of creaking muscles. The drizzle sifted down. The beam of the torch, wavering over the pathway, picked out boulders and stones in seemingly endless procession, or, as a stumble sent it shooting sideways over the edge, snuffed softly out into black velvet, swallowed by three-dimensional darkness. The angle slackened. A gate appeared. At eleven o'clock we tumbled into the tent.

The rest was tragedy, taken neat. Jake collapsed

slowly on to the floor of the tent, dribbling rain and snow, and caring for nothing but that he be called upon to make no further effort in any direction. I had to wake him to get him out of his wet clothes, whereupon he fell asleep again, naked and steaming on the floor, and had to be put to bed like an infant. He was dead beat and past thinking of food. By the time I had changed my own clothes and lit the stove, the tent was heaped high with wet garments. Trousers, clammy and repulsive to the touch though we had worn them only a few minutes before, blocked the door. The nails of four boots caught from opposing corners of the tent the light of our single candle. Underwear was mixed with our pots and pans. And from the heap, steam arose. Small tents have their disadvantages.

It was while I was rummaging through this midden for the food that I noticed a piece of rhubarb on Jake's sleeping-bag.

" Now, that's curious," I thought. " That should be inside a rhubarb tart."

I looked for the tart, and it was not there. A horrid suspicion began to dawn. I threw wet clothes about and searched the tent from one end to the other. Still the tart was not there. And neither were the sausages, nor the bread, nor the scones, nor the four beautiful chops I had been building castles in the air about for three hours. The tent, so far as food was concerned, was a dead loss. A dog from the farm had broken in and eaten the lot.

From a large repertoire of miserable moments I cannot think of one worse. The subject was not inherently dramatic ; but dramatists have always had a soft spot in their hearts and plots for the lusts of the flesh, and that night I lusted after four pork chops with an abandon which would have shamed Tarquin. Outside, the gale raged ; inside, the clothes steamed. The only food in the tent was tinned beans, and I had no tin-opener. Jake slept like an unsympathetic log. I very nearly wept.

IV

Act Three opened in a beach shelter on the south side of Fort William. We had risen late, bought milk and eggs and borrowed a tin-opener at the farm, and made ourselves a meal. Thereafter we wandered slowly to Fort William and sought out the lorry driver ; but, as he ostentatiously failed to recognise us, we concluded that the man he was talking to was his employer, and lay low until he was alone. His news, when he spoke to us, was bad. When the breakdown van had attempted to drag the lorry clear of the drainage system of Ballachulish, the cargo had toppled overboard, twisting the chassis as it fell. The lorry was out of action, but another one had been commandeered to take its place, and should be leaving within the hour. And would we please keep clear of the garage, as the boss's temper was a fair caution, and had to be seen to be believed. We slipped out like conspirators and headed for the shelter, where, said the driver, he would collect us.

That had been at four o'clock. It was now seven o'clock, and there was still no sign of the lorry. The shelter, of a type common at seaside resorts, was shaped like a cross, and the alcoves set between its arms were open to the four winds of heaven, one of which was blasting its way across Loch Linnhe and making life all but insupportable in three of the alcoves. We sat in the centre of the fourth, and sheltered, side, thereby making ourselves exceedingly unpopular with all the courting couples of Fort William, for it was black night and Sunday night, and Fort William is a well-lit place at the best of times, besides being windy. Here was shelter and blessed darkness, and we were in it. Hints, to the effect that some folk ought to play the game, were passed in the draughtier sections of the shelter, but we refused to hear them. We sat grimly on while the swains of Fort William, their passion impervious to weather, kissed their best girls to left and right of us. No one, so far as I know, braved the side which faced into the teeth of the wind. Hard things were said in our direction as each couple left.

The lorry arrived out of the darkness at nine o'clock and stood panting by the shelter. It was empty and without a tarpaulin. We lay on the open back for thirty miles, with the rain lashing down and no shelter whatever, bounding and roaring through the night with moist, heavy trees and sodden walls flying behind us, and a well-planned system of pot-holes demonstrating with the aid of the lightly-laden lorry and our protesting carcases the vividness and aptness of the simile about the pea in the drum. It was horrid.

Jake weathered the storm like a Spartan, but it was more than I could stand. My sleeping-bag, which still had pungent memories of sheep lingering in it, was of eiderdown and lightweight cotton, and was by no means waterproof; but it was better than nothing. I crawled inside it, raincoat, boots, and all, and spent the rest of the journey in trying to protect it with a groundsheet. This was ticklish in the extreme. It involved, every now and then, touching my toes while in a sitting position in order to hook the end of the sheet under my heels, for the wind kept tearing it free, spilling puddles over the eiderdown and converting the groundsheet itself into a slimy, flapping horror. Invariably, we passed over a pot-hole at speed at the critical moment when both my hands were engaged and my only points of contact with the floor were the seat of my trousers and the tips of my heels, whereupon the lorry left me, returned suddenly, rapped me smartly on the seat like a spring-board, and shot me an inch or two into the air. Three times I was fielded by Jake just as I was disappearing sideways into the outer darkness. It was not a pleasant journey.

Fortunately, at the end of thirty miles, the driver dropped the two friends who had been sharing the cab with him, and we sat inside for the rest of the way. At 3 a.m. on the following morning, to the surprise of such neighbours as were wakened by the clatter, I was driven in state to my front door, and said good-bye to Jake. I have not seen him since, and am not so sure that I want to.

I have several vivid memories of him—shouting in the dark among the sheep, reading his enormous compass on the mountain, and tottering down the last long slope in his sleep. But the most vivid memory of them all is an incident on the lorry during the liquid thirty miles before we were allowed inside the driver's cab. He was hunched up inside a spare tyre, the sole cargo, with his teeth rattling every time we jumped a pot-hole, and rain pouring in a continuous stream off the brim of his hat. His lips were numb; and he turned to me and summed up the whole week-end neatly and concisely in one sentence.

" D'you know," said Jake, " we're daft."

I still think he was right. That was the first and last time I joined the ranks of the hitch-hikers.

CHAPTER SIX

THE BERRY-PICKING

WINTER passed, the Spring snow melted, and there came a day when I met four flatties sitting by the roadside near Blairgowrie, boiling tea after a day at the berry-picking. It was a hot day, and a blue haze lay over the dusty roads and miles of raspberry fields which cover the Carse of Gowrie. The roads were busy, for the Tinkers' Parliament was sitting.

There are three classes of professional nomads on the Scottish roads—the flatties, the minks, and the haakers. The flatties are tramps ; men who, born in houses, have taken to the road. The minks are low-class tinkers. And the haakers—or hawkers—are aristocrat tinkers, kings of the road with a clan system as detailed and complicated as any in Debrett. When July comes and the raspberries ripen, these three groups of people descend on Blairgowrie from the ends of Scotland, there to pick raspberries for a ha'penny a pound and meet their friends.

The flatties attend or do not attend, as the mood takes them, for their magnet is money and the berries are a chance to pick up an honest penny which they may or may not want ; but the others, the minks and the haakers, will allow only sickness or infirmity to come between them and the berry-fields, for there they take part in what would be to any other body of people a national re-union. They come in carts with tiny ponies in front and half a dozen children bringing up the rear. They come in decrepit motor cars heaped high with brooms and baskets. They come with little hand-carts piled full of rags, jam jars, and scrap. They come in caravans, and they come on the flats of their feet. Blairgowrie in July is the rallying-ground of every tinker, man, woman, and child, who tramps the roads of Scotland.

I was not due back in Glasgow for three days and had no plans when I turned off the main road and took to the cart-track which straggled through the berry-fields, thinking that I might come on a place where I might pitch my tent. When I had walked half a mile I met the four flatties. The oldest looked about forty and the youngest cannot have been a day older than twenty. They were all what Mr. Wodehouse would call ten-minute eggs, and they were engaged in boiling tea in an old five-pound coffee tin they had found in a ditch somewhere. They asked me if I should like some, and I said I should. We talked. I left them three days later.

Those week-enders who spend all their nights in hostels learn much about human nature and about a diversity of jobs ; but, wide though the social canvas of the hostels is, it has its limitations. Those four would never have been found in a hostel, and they were four I should not willingly have missed.

They were fair representatives of their class. First, there was Forfar. He was so called because he came from Forfar, or said he did ; and no one, not even his friends of the moment, knew his real name, though it is not beyond the bounds of possibility that the police did. He gave me the impression that he was on the road because the cities were too hot for him. He was small, dark, broad in the shoulder, and had a scar, newly healed, over one eye. He talked little; but he did mention one night that he had acquired the scar in a fight, and could have licked the man who did it with one hand if only he had been sober when he was struck. A soup-plate, it seemed, had been the weapon.

Second, there was Jock, also dark, wiry, and rather chipped about the face. He was swarthier than Forfar. He was half-tinker—on his mother's side—but a mink so seldom marries outside the clan that Jock was really in a class by himself. He was on the road because he had been brought up to it, which a flattie practically never is. His father had been Irish, and from him he had inherited the gift of the gab, which must have tried his mother sorely, for a talkative mink is a contradiction in terms and he talked more than any twenty minks I ever met. But, unlike most talkers, he was a mighty man in a fight.

Third, there was Admiral Charlie, a trawlerman who took to the road between-times. He was on his way to Fleetwood to look for a job, but showed such a notable disinclination to stir a foot that he clearly did not care if the entire herring fleet sank before he got there. He was long and lanky, with straight, greying hair which hung low on his forehead and a complexion of that peculiar reddish-brown which comes from the sea. He smoked a very short pipe, clamped in one of his enormous hands. His face, like the rest of him, was long; and the furrows in it were deep. He spoke seldom and slowly. He had an extraordinary knack for finding golf balls, and had spent a delightful month sleeping in a wood near Nairn every night and scouring the local course for balls by day. His average bag was about two dozen ; and Jock who had seen him at work, swore he could smell them. However, after a while the police had become unreasonable, and Charlie had drifted south to Blairgowrie.

And fourth was Harry, ex-newsboy and boxer, and the decentest flattie I ever met. He had been a newsboy in Aberdeen ; but, after a series of battles waged in the less pleasant places in the city and too complicated for me to follow, had lost his pitch and taken to tramping. He was twenty years old, fit as a fiddle, a bundle of muscle, and living, with the other three, in an old mattress slit round three sides, with gussets of tablecloth sewn in at the ends with string to make a cottage-tent.

The day, as I have said, was hot and hazy ; and the spell of good weather which had preceded it showed no signs of breaking. The berry-picking had been abandoned, for dry berries are less in weight and bulk than wet ones, and the farmers preferred to wait until rain should fall. So we lay on our backs in the sun, and talked, and ate raspberries, and talked, and ate raspberries, and talked. Around us were the long, straight drills of raspberry canes, stretching in a dusty green carpet almost to the range of hills on the horizon. There was silence, except for the clanking of an occasional cart and a burst of concertina music borne on the haze from a distant camp. Occasionally, too, some one would walk slowly down the cart-track—a boy sent to the farm for milk, a family of Glasgow folk who hoped to make their holiday pay, a student from one of

the farms which recruited pickers from the universities.
a tinker woman. No one did anything in a hurry. It
was all very peaceful.

I pitched my tent beside the mattress, and took
Harry in beside me. It seemed best to do this, because
four men to a mattress, even in dry weather, scarcely
makes for comfort, and I had room enough for two.
Harry was touched. He said he would repay me with
boxing lessons, which promise he fulfilled so earnestly
that I was black and blue for a fortnight. When we
bedded down that first night, I found that he, too,
belonged to the brown paper school, but favoured a
mixture of sacking and back numbers of the *Scotsman*
for the upper layers of blankets. After much rustling,
we fell asleep.

Next morning I walked to the ramshackle store
which someone had built beside the track, and bought
breakfast, which was cooked by the Admiral over a
wood fire expertly lit and tended by Forfar. We had
sausages and eggs, and by the time we had finished them
the sun was sufficiently high to allow us to continue our
sunbathe. We lay in great contentment.

" I'm sorry I forgot to buy jam," I said. " We
could have polished off that loaf if we'd had something
to help it down."

The Admiral shuddered. " Jam ? " he said.
" God forbid ! "

" Don't you like jam ? " I asked.

" We do nut." The Admiral was emphatic.

" O' course, ye wouldna ken aboot that," said
Jock, who took pride in schooling me in these matters,
" but no flattie on this earth ever did like jam. No sir.
Noo, ye're a flattie, and ye're hungry, see ? And ye go

to tap a jigger . . . sorry, go to knock at a door . . . to try for a handoot, see ? And the wifie comes to the door, and she looks at ye, and ye say ye're hungry. And she looks at ye again, and ye try to look as if ye hadna seen a square meal this side o' Christmas. And she goes to get ye some chuck, see ? And what does she bring ye, eh ? What does she bring ye ? She brings ye a jam piece, that's what she brings ye, two big slabs o' breed wi' a slather o' jam in atween ! "

" Every time ? "

" Ay. Every time. We ca' them Dundee Sandwiches, and unless we're fair desperate we heave them ower the first dyke we come to."

" They're no' safe," said Forfar morosely, breaking his usual silence. " I got jiled once that way. The polis foond them in ma pocket."

" But the woman gave them to you. It wasn't stealing."

" Oh, ay. She gi'ed them to me all right. That was the trouble. I was clinked for vagrancy. Fourteen days. Anyone that looks like a flattie that's foond wi' Dundee Sandwiches in his pocket is as guid as clinked. The polis thinks they're a sort o' flattie's trade-mark." He looked gloomily over the berry-drills, and spat. " And they're no' far wrang, either," he said.

About eleven o'clock I thought I had better bestir myself and go to buy lunch. There was nothing unreasonable in my providing for them, because they were an entertaining crowd and I was enjoying myself ; but when they heard I was going to the store again they would have none of it. I had provided breakfast : it was their turn now.

" Well, I don't want to be personal, or anything

like that," I said, " but there's been no picking for two days and it was poor going before then. Not to put too fine a point on it, have you any money ? "

" Have we any money ! " Harry was scornful. He held out his hand, and in the palm of it was a sixpence. The other three had a penny between them.

" Eh . . . yes," I said, " but . . . I mean . . . sevenpence. There *are* five of us, you know."

Harry said that if five could not have a slap-up meal for sevenpence, his technique was slipping. The four arose and sauntered off up the cart-track towards Blairgowrie, the Admiral slouching in a sleepy way he had, Harry and Forfar with an aggressive swing to their shoulders, and Jock waving his hands as he launched another story. I wondered how far sevenpence would go in a small town which had been begged dry for a fortnight by three thousand tramps and tinkers. I had just decided that it might buy two loaves, when I fell asleep.

Three hours later I was shaken into wakefulness by Harry's foot, with which he was prodding my shoulder. He could not use his hands, because they held the spoils. When I was fully awake, but not before, he laid them on the ground in front of me, and the others added their burdens to the pile. The two loaves were there : so far I had been right. But with them were a pound of butter, a packet of biscuits, half a dozen scones, a small packet of tea and another of sugar, and five smoked haddocks.

" How on earth . . ." I began.

" Oh, and I forgot something," said Harry, delving into his pocket and holding out his hand. In the palm was a sixpence. And Forfar, grinning, was spinning a penny into the air.

I asked no questions after that. I thought that, on the whole, it might be as well to ask none. It was a very good lunch.

II

Life at Blairgowrie was not without its excitement, thanks mainly to the peculiar sense of humour which afflicted Harry and his friends. Along the cart-track passed many of the tougher citizens of Scotland, male and female ; and it seemed to me that Harry's habit of leaning out of the tent as each female passed and shouting the catch-word of the moment, which was " Come up and see me sometime," was nothing short of courting disaster. Anyone will agree with this conclusion who has heard the fine flow of vituperation commanded by the average female mink in her cups, or knows the habit these ladies have of setting the clan on those who have caused them displeasure.

There was one mink encampment in particular which I avoided carefully for two of the three days I spent in the berry-fields. One of its more prominent members was a lady of unknown age but formidable physique who had a very small husband and a taste for gin. This much I learned from Jock, who knew everyone. My first sight of the lady was on the evening of the second day, when she came ramping down the cart-track, far gone in liquor and followed by her husband, a miserable specimen half her size who had also drink taken.

" Come up and see me sometime," shouted Harry in a very suggestive manner indeed.

The woman stopped on the other side of the wire

fence which separated us from the track, rocking on her heels and pushing with one hand her tangle of hair into even wilder disarray. There was battle in her eye. She was a very big woman.

" Wha' was that you said ? "

" Come up and see me sometime, dearie," said Harry.

The woman considered this carefully, her lips moving to the words. At last it sank in.

" God ! " she said. " I'm insulted ! "

The wandering hands slammed down to her hips, and stayed there. Still rocking, she told us precisely what she thought of us, and what her people would do when she reported to them fully how grievous were the insults she had undergone. Gutting, it seemed, was too good for us ; and ham-stringing was childish. With much picturesque detail, for there was nothing niggardly about her style, she heaped point upon point and adjective upon coloured adjective until every cane in Blairgowrie should by rights have been blighted. As she fetched breath for a fresh onslaught, Harry said :

" So you're not coming up ? "

She took it in silence, bottling her wrath, until it escaped in one thunderous word in the direction of her husband, at that moment having trouble with a ditch.

" John ! "

The bellow had no effect, for it was a complicated ditch, and John was at the stage of inebriation when all his powers of concentration and ingenuity had to be bent to solving the simplest of problems.

" John ! Come here, you lout. Come here and show these . . ."

But John had decided that little was to be gained

by further effort, and had subsided into the ditch. She reeled towards him, hurling abuse at us over her shoulder. Stepping down into the ditch, she hoisted him bodily on to the road and dragged him back towards us.

" If you're a man," she roared, " you'll not stand by and let your wife be insulted."

It was entirely a coincidence that John ceased to stand then, but wilted slowly like a badly stuffed pillow and curled up in a little heap on the road. From that moment onwards she forgot us. She grabbed him by the collar, hauled him to his feet, and shook him till his eyes turned inwards and I thought his neck would break. Harry watched, appalled. She roared abuse, in her rage forgetting the original cause of it, until in the end, losing patience with her now three-parts unconscious man, she lugged him off down the track towards their camp, still lashing him with her tongue. Long after they had passed out of sight round the bend we could hear sudden torrents of speech across the berry-drills, until even they were lost in the distance, and there was silence.

" And let that be a lesson to you," said Harry, for no reason at all that I could see.

We never saw them again, so the woman must have been too drunk to remember the incident when she came to next morning. Still, I kept clear of her camp. You cannot be too careful about these things.

III

Harry and I were fighting. The other three had gone off to search for food, and Harry had decided it was high time he paid for his night's lodging. For ten minutes we had been circling round a little square of grass among the berries.

"No, no. Keep that left shoulder o' yours *forward*," he was saying. "Oh, man, man, there ye go again! Ye've left yer chin wide open. Cover up, man, cover up! Thaaat's it." He dropped his hands, and looked at me seriously. "Ay, ye're comin' on no' so bad; but watch that left o' yours."

I stood and panted. Harry was gentle as a mother; but it was exhausting work.

"Now," said Harry, who was not even warm, "Ye'd better be learnin' the screw. Mind ye, I'm no' suggestin' ye should foul deliberate; but ye'd be as well to ken how it's done in case the ither fella starts the dirty work. Now, screwin' yer punches takes the skin aff of the ither fella, and ye can use yer elbows on the ref's blind side. Like this . . ."

Harry spoke with enthusiasm, a smile on his battered face, happy to be of service to a stranger. There was just such an expression on the face of the aircraft designer who once explained to me how his new flying-boats would cut days off the Karachi run. It was the eager smile of the expert lost in his subject. When he had finished, we lay on the grass and talked of boxing and other things. I heard what it feels like to become a professional boxer at sixteen, and exactly what mixture of tact and brute force (the first for the police, the second for other newsboys) is required to hold a street-corner pitch in the newsvending business. I learned of the towns in which the police deal least kindly with vagrants, and that, when "tapping" doors, one should always call first on the local minister. Then Harry told me a story.

Harry had lost his pitch. He had had three non-professional fights and had quarrelled with the police all in one week, and financially he was on the rocks. So when a man came along and offered him twelve shillings a week for selling firewood from a barrow, he accepted.

" He made a fine skin aff it," said Harry. " He picked up the wood for next to nothin', and sold it at tuppence a bundle. Anither fella got a bob a hundred-weight for choppin' it. He must have skinned near four bob a hundredweight, clear."

From Monday until Saturday he pushed his barrow round the streets of Aberdeen, and by the end of the week had more than earned his wages. He was therefore pardonably annoyed when his employer refused to pay up. The position was interesting. His employer (whom we shall call Smith for want of his real name) was entirely without scruples, and imagined that Harry was receiving unemployment benefit at the time. If this had been the case, Harry should have reported to the local Labour Exchange when he found work, otherwise he would have been defrauding the Government by earning money while he was being paid to earn nothing.

So this unpleasant Mr. Smith simply said : " Na, na. Ye'll get naethin' oot o' me. Whit would the Burroo man say if I tellt him ye wis makin' a bit of money on the sly ? "

Harry, surprisingly enough, suffered him to live. It seemed he wanted to plan his campaign before committing himself, although he knew that, as he was receiving no Dole, he could earn what he liked without transgressing the law. While selling papers he had been his own master, and had not been insured. He was not eligible for Dole.

However, instead of resorting immediately to violence, he went to the Labour Exchange and had ten minutes' talk with the clerk there.

"Jist to get legal advice on the matter, like," he explained to me.

And having obtained all the information he wanted, and put it, as he said, on a sound legal footing, he set up a little blackmailing business on his own account.

He sought out the clever Mr. Smith and said: "I don't want twelve shillings."

"Want it or not," said Mr. Smith, "ye're no' gettin' twelve shillings."

"No," said Harry, "I'm gettin' twenty-four shillings; and if I dinna get it, I'm goin' to the polis. Ye're my employer, and because ye're my employer ye should have stamped an insurance card for me. That's the law. And ye havena done it. And the fines ye get for no' puttin' on stamps is somethin' terrible. Come on. Twenty-four shillings, or I'll have the polis on ye."

Mr. Smith, it appeared, loved money above all things and, even when the full horror of the situation had dawned upon him, was more inclined to fight than pay. There was no honesty in the world, he said. Twenty-four shillings was a great deal of money, and he would rot in prison before he parted with it to so low a thing as Harry. In the end he stalked off with the injured expression of one whose cutlery has been stolen by the waif he saved from the gutter. On no account, he said, would he pay. Harry shouted after him that he had until ten o'clock that night to disgorge: after that he was going to the police.

Now Harry was staying with another newsboy in a single room ; and the pair of them waited for Mr. Smith, who arrived at nine-thirty, cut to the quick and using naughty language, but with twenty-four shillings in hard cash. This he handed over with very bad grace ; and, abandoning his injured gentleman role and throwing restraint to the winds, let loose a flow of language which shocked even Harry. And when Harry is shocked, it means a fight.

Nor was Mr. Smith averse to battle. The tirade, it seemed, had worked him up to a fine fever, and finished with : " And if ye step doon to the lane, I'll show ye whether ye can rob an honest man of twenty-four bob, you . . ."

This was an offer truly generous. Harry, being, as I have said, shocked, replied that nothing, positively nothing, would give him greater pleasure ; and he was half-way to the door before his friend could catch his arm and haul him back. Harry protested ; but Mr. Smith left alone.

" Come here," said his friend when he had gone, leading Harry to the window. " Look."

Below the window was a lamp, and below the lamp was an under-sized individual who was not Mr. Smith.

" Well, what about it ? " said Harry. " I could have lickit the both of them, easy."

" Ay. But he's no' there to fight. He's a witness."

" A witness for what ? "

" A witness for the court case o' assault ye'd have landed yersel' in if ye'd gone doonstairs the now."

Harry and I stared over the berry-drills in silence for a while. A woman went to the store, and a party of mink children passed down the track, singing. At last Harry sighed.

"But och, man, I was a fool. I could have got two quid off him, easy."

IV

One last word about Harry. He told me he was saving up to get married. I asked him how much he needed, and he said ten shillings.

"Ten shillings more ? " I asked.

"No," said Harry, "ten shillings altogether. The licence costs seven-and-six, and I ken a place where ye can get married for half-a-croon. That makes ten shillings."

I asked him how he meant to live after that.

"Och, we'll manage," he said.

That story still sounds far-fetched : it seemed even more so, at the time. I thought he wanted ten shillings, and imagined that the marriage yarn might open my pocket.

Well, it did. We had been together for three days, and he, and Forfar, and the Admiral, and Jock had entertained me like old friends. So on the morning when I left, after they had escorted me to the 'bus stop at the end of the road, I handed Harry a ten-shilling note.

Harry refused to take it.

CHAPTER SEVEN

BUCK ISLAND

I WAS driving down the West Highland road when I came on a car which I knew belonged to a friend of mine, a man much given to running up and down mountains. It was standing by the roadside a few miles south of Tyndrum, at that point where the road swings to the right and crosses the big bridge ; and that struck me as curious, because the car was empty and there was no mountain within striking distance except Beinn Chaluim, an uninspiring slag-heap of a hill on which few mountaineers would think of spending their time.

So I stopped and looked for my friend, knowing he could not be far away. Eventually I saw him. He was half a mile off, in the middle of that tangle of bog and heather and ancient morain heaps which lie west of the road at that point ; and he was behaving in an extraordinary manner. First he ran in one direction, and cast himself flat on his face. Then he rose, as if he intended running again, but suddenly changed his mind and dropped once more. Then he was away in the opposite direction, and the whole performance was repeated.

This I watched for perhaps five minutes, and could make nothing of it. After that he stopped hopping about, and walked back to the car in a perfectly rational way. When he reached me he seemed well pleased with himself and with the world ; and the only explanation of his behaviour which he deemed it necessary to offer was that he had seen a heron. That was all. He had just seen a heron.

So I thought that one day it might be interesting to discover what it was that made otherwise normal human beings lose all sense of proportion when birds were mentioned ; but it was no more than a passing thought, and it died, as these fancies do, as soon as something else arrived to distract my attention. That would have been the end of the matter if I had not met this man in town some months later, and he had not remarked in an excessively cheerful tone of voice that the terns would be nesting by now.

" Let me understand you," I said. " The terns are nesting, and you are very pleased about it. No one has left you a fortune. You aren't getting married. The terns are just nesting. That's all. You're sure there isn't something you've forgotten to tell me ? "

" No," said he. " Why should there be ? Nesting terns are dashed interesting, and I happen to be studying them. You'd be quite cock-a-hoop yourself if you'd waited all winter for them to arrive, and then heard that the eggs were appearing."

So it was that, two days later, he and I and another man who was a species of apprentice bird-watcher foregathered on a spit of land on the shore of Loch Fyne, and looked first at Buck Island, which lay a hundred and fifty yards away across the water, and second at one of the smallest and leakiest boats I have ever clapped eyes on. It was a close, heavy day in summer, dry and windless ; and nothing but a few gulls stirred on all the coast, where the sea was separated from the heather by only a few feet of barnacle-covered

rock. Even the gulls were silent. The only sound was
the barking of a dog, miles away on the far side of the
loch. The place was a desert of rock, heather, and salt
water ; and the only sign of man's work in the whole
vast landscape was the boat.

We launched the boat. Water immediately
spouted through its seams in a score of generous jets,
whereupon my friend looked at it with a calculating
eye and announced that I should have to swim. It
was a peculiar sort of boat, he said. It held only two ;
and, even with that slight cargo, it took years to master
the art of rowing without capsizing, and years more to
learn to bale at such a rate that the output equalled
the intake. He could row, and the apprentice bird-
watcher could bale. And he was afraid I could
swim.

The procession of three set off. First went the
tiny boat, with the bird-watcher and his assistant face
to face, knees touching, backs hard against bow and
stern, looking absurdly like twins in a home-made
perambulator. One rowed in short, jerky strokes—
there was not space for more—while the other, fighting
a losing battle against the encroaching sea, sent a large
tin mug flying back and forth from the gaping bilges
to the gunwale. Creaking and protesting, the boat
waddled out into Loch Fyne, with myself spluttering
in its wake. What with the splashes from the toy oars,
the erratic aim of the baler, and the fact that no single
man, however well trained, could keep pace with the
leaks, the boat was awash and I as dry as anyone by the
time we grounded on Buck Island.

The first thing I noticed when I had dressed was
the noise. Before, there had been silence ; but now

the air was white with screaming gulls vastly agitated and yelling bloody murder, swooping and interweaving, diving at our heads and panicking back to the sky as their courage failed them at the last moment. There was terror there, and anger, and flashing white wings against the thundery sky. There were hundreds of them. One particularly big gull was bawling, " Help, help, help ! " at the pitch of its voice, startlingly human against the raucous background. My friend smiled, and said it was the biggest bully of them all. It was a great blackbacked gull, a villainous pirate of a bird with a wing-span of several feet and a habit of swallowing smaller gulls whole.

By this time I could see that the island was not more than two hundred yards across, and made up mainly of bare rock and coarse grass. A few feet lower, and it would have been a tidal skerry, too washed by the waves to grow more than seaweed. Yet, though it was no bigger than a garden, it was the home of hundreds of birds. I do not think I have ever seen so many concentrated on one spot, except at Mallaig or Wick when the herring fleet was in and thousands of gulls were fighting for the scraps. But there was no herring fleet here. So I asked my friend why Loch Fyne should be so popular, and he pointed to the atrocious state of the road by which we had travelled from Glasgow, and to the absence of other roads in the district.

" Good ground for nesting, and uninhabited country," he said. " There are dozens of little islands like this round about here, all of them good for sea-birds ; but if they made a road along the coast they'd all be away in a few years. It's the same on

Loch Lomond, only they're mainly inland birds there. On the west shore of the loch, where the road is, there are very few. But on the other side, where the road stops short at Rowardennan and leaves miles of untouched country, you'll find thousands of all sorts. And the Loch Lomond islands are the same. They're rarely visited, and so they've become bird sanctuaries."

There was a sparkle in his eye as he said this, Harry the Flattie all over again in his enthusiasm. Here, evidently, was bird-watching rampant. He was a dark, lean man, not normally given much to talking, but apt to be drawn out of himself by his subject. Then there was no stopping him, nor did anyone ever want to stop him. He put life into it. He made breathing birds from words. And then he would smile apologetically, and become silent once more. That day on Buck Island his whole body was curiously alert, and there was a spring in his step. Somehow, he was strangely bird-like himself.

He walked on ahead of me, moving fast, but making little noise. Suddenly he stooped, and picked up the empty shell of a crab.

" Well ? " I said.

He pointed to other shells lying at our feet, and said : " There's a nest here, obviously."

He was right. It was hidden in some bracken ; but the shells gave it away. It was a common gull's nest, with four eggs in it. The eggs were a brownish olive-green, with brown spots like newly fallen raindrops. He picked one up.

" Won't the birds abandon the nest if you do that ? " I asked.

" No. Seagulls aren't fussy. I *think* this is a

common gull's nest; but hold on a second and I'll make sure."

He looked at the sky for a few seconds in a way that was natural, and unstudied, and competent, and then announced that he had been right. It was quite easy when you knew the trick. Of all the hundreds of gulls flying above us, one was swooping much lower than the rest and seemed twice as indignant.

"It'll probably take another day yet to break its way out," he said, dispassionately. He had handed me the egg, which I nearly dropped, for it chirped. "And some of the bigger ones . . . these black-backs, for instance . . . sometimes take three days. All chicks have a little knob on top of their beaks to help them peck their way out, you know. It disappears when they grow up. Look. You'll see it on that one."

I could see no chick; but he dived under a ledge and produced one with such dexterity that I began to see Buck Island as an immense conjurer's hat. When he pointed them out I could see three others, fluffy little things without real feathers, merging quietly into the heather and lichen-covered rocks. The first chick was a trifle sulky, but did not appear to mind being made the subject of a natural history lesson; and I duly saw the knob growing from the top of its beak like an immature rhinoceros's horn. When we put it back under its ledge, the chick turned its back on us and glowered over its shoulder.

"Now come to the top of the island, and we'll talk," said the bird-watcher.

We sat on the great boulder which was the island's highest point, and, while the seagulls screamed and we gazed along the deserted coast-line, he told me all about it.

People, it seems, generally start bird-watching
unintentionally, through some other sport. They may
fish, or shoot, or walk, or climb hills ; and while they
are doing so they cannot avoid noticing a bird every
now and then. The angler probably comes to know
that amusing one with the white waistcoat which flies
for a short distance and then bobs up and down on a
stone in midstream. He may not know its name, but
he grows to know the bird itself. He may even be
lucky, and see a king-fisher.

Or he may be a climber, in which case he soon
learns that a ptarmigan will allow a man to approach it
closely before it flies away, and that ravens and hoody
crows live on cliffs and sound, in mist, like the souls of
the damned. And he will see several eagles. Then
the day will come when he sees a real eagle and realises
that what he saw before were buzzards, and that never
in his life will he make the same mistake again, because
the eagle has the most arrogant and beautiful flight of
any British bird.

And then he begins to notice particular and
unusual things which birds do, like the tremendous
flying of feathers and croaks of laughter I came on in
the Cuillin when two hoody crows were engaged in
knocking the stuffing out of a young eagle which
finished by flying away very quickly and not in the
least arrogantly ; or the two black-headed gulls, also
in the Cuillin, which at one time followed climbers along
the ridges to catch the scraps from their lunches, just
as other gulls follow ships for the same purpose.

And then . . . and then he dashes hot-foot to the
nearest shop and spends far more than he intended on a
pair of binoculars. Gently, insidiously as carbon

monoxide gas, bird-watching has crept up behind him and gained possession of his pocket and his reason. He begins to flop in bogs when he sees herons.

Then, said the bird-watcher, the true fascination of the game is revealed to anyone with eyes sufficiently clear of city smoke to see. After the obvious things, such as the fact that most birds in flight are lovely things to watch, and that a bird seen through binoculars is not an uneasy creature with one eye on you all the time, you discover that the different varieties have different habits, and that even individual birds may have mannerisms of their own. Instead of seeing *an* oyster-catcher, you see *the* oyster-catcher you noticed the day before yesterday. You discover that individual birds have their own little corner of the wood or beach, and often have set routes from twig to twig or from stone to stone—always the same twigs and the same stones—like the tracks of rabbits in a field. Only birds do not wear a track in the grass as rabbits do, and so you did not notice before. You can identify birds with your eyes shut, because you know their songs. You learn the different nesting seasons, and know almost to a day (because you have been watching the weather for weeks beforehand) when certain migratory birds will reach this country. But most of all you learn that if you sit still and watch a bird, preferably through a pair of good binoculars, you find that it is a surprisingly individual creature with habits you want to know more about.

" And that," said the bird-watcher, " is why I stalk herons and feel cheerful when the terns are nesting. Silly, isn't it ? "

We sat watching the gulls for a little while, and then I pottered about on my own, and found an eider-duck's nest, and felt hugely pleased with myself. The disease had not bitten me (and still has not, though there is plenty of time yet) ; but I remembered things which had happened, and thought I could see the fascination of it.

There was the day when I saw my first eagle. It happened when Sandy, and William, and John, and I set out on our first Skye climb and crawled up the Window Buttress. We were perched on the uttermost tip of the pinnacle above the Window when it came sailing across the corrie, about a mile away and coming straight towards us. In all the time we saw it, it did not move its wings, but only the long feathers at the tips, which it held splayed out like fingers, catching every stray current of air and adjusting its balance to it. It was supremely indifferent to us ; and it soared past only thirty feet away. We saw every feather. It was tremendous. It was a great experience. But it would not have made a bird-watcher of me or of anyone else.

What might very easily have done that was an incident which happened that day on Buck Island by the shore of Loch Fyne. I had the binoculars, and I was watching, not a spectacular bird like an eagle, but a couple of oyster-catchers, which are dissipated looking creatures which make a noise like a squeaky door and practically never catch oysters. They are not in the least impressive. They are gawky, with rather silly red beaks and legs. I watched this pair for ten minutes or so, and in that time they had become almost characters. They had a curious, jerky way of walking, like a footman with his elbows out ; and they had a mild sort of quarrel, in which one pretended to peck the other but obviously really did not mean to, and the other one ran away a few paces. And then they made it up, and padded solemnly about among the rocks, picking up odds and ends. That was all. There were no tremendous flights, no impressiveness, nothing like that. But in spite of myself I found that I wanted to know more about them—what they ate, which birds they bullied and which ones they avoided, and how two such apparently unhandy creatures could contrive to rear a family.

And by the grin on the bird-watcher's face, I could see he knew what I was thinking.

He was talking about egg-sellers when we left the island (I exploded the baling theory and made the apprentice bird-watcher swim back), men who ignore the protection laws and steal eggs for those extraordinary people who must collect something— ebony elephants, or butterflies, or public notices, or door-knockers—and happen to collect birds' eggs, which is just about as pointless a proceeding as I know, though a profitable one for the poachers who supply the eggs at double the price they charged in the days before taking eggs was illegal. My friend was not fond of these gentlemen or their customers. He had found his tern's nest—a little hollow in the turf, with some smallish eggs in it—and he knew that soon the poachers would be sneaking out to the islands of Loch Lomond, where many terns nest, and clearing them all.

The apprentice bird-watcher dried himself and we went home, I with my mind much exercised over the price of binoculars, and the bird-watcher talking of some plan to maroon himself on an island near Cape Wrath. It seemed there were puffins there. Puffins were interesting creatures. I would like them.

I shifted a little uneasily in my seat. I had no desire to go to Cape Wrath; and yet . . . Bird-watching, I decided, was too infectious to be comfortable.

CHAPTER EIGHT

DAN MACKAY'S BARN

THE wind had been rising all afternoon, bringing with it sheets of rain and mist which crept uneasily lower and lower down the hillsides ; and when the wind rose to gale force as night came on, I knew that summer was over. The night was vile, and I was glad to make the most I could of Dan Mackay's fire, heaped high with red logs, before the moment came when I should have to open the door and scuttle fifty yards along the road to the barn.

I was living in the barn. To have slept at an hotel would have cost me at least eight shillings ; and eight shillings added to the twelve and six I had paid in 'bus fares would have pushed the expense of my week-end beyond the bounds of extravagance into the realms of absurdity. A pound was a great deal of money : I could have had two week-ends at Arrochar for less. Unfortunately, however, I had spent most week-ends for a year at Arrochar, and of late had become increasingly aware that most of the climbing stories I had heard had been set in Glencoe. Hence the twelve and sixpenny 'bus fare. Also mentioned in these stories had been the barn of one Daniel Mackay. Hence the fact that my rucksack at that moment was balanced on a pile of hay just beyond reach of two tough little ponies lately employed in bringing gralloched stags off the hill. Of Hamish, whom I had expected to find with the ponies, there was no sign.

I had been wet, and Mrs. Mackay had taken pity on me. So I sat by her kitchen fire and smoked, while Dan talked of stags, and poachers, and the fifteen hundred navvies who once had built the Blackwater Dam, four miles behind us up the hill.

" Eh, but they were the wild ones, the navvies," said Dan. " It was like yon stories you read about the gold-rushes in the Yukon. Dam't man, there was no law in the camp—only three bobbies down at Kinloch-leven, four miles away ; and did the bobbies ever look near the camp ? They did not. And they were wise."

That was in 1905. Dan was in his forties then, living in that same cottage of Alltnafeidh, at the mouth of Glencoe. He was a stalker on Strathcona's estate in those days : he was head stalker when I first knew him, still fit for a day on the hill in the wildest of weather. He had been up that afternoon. He sat stretched out in his chair, his stalker's spats half into the fire, the red glow catching his craggy old face and magnificent moustachios. Two dogs lay beside him, and a rack of guns gleamed in a far corner.

" You'll have read Pat McGill's *Children of the Dead End* ? " he said.

I said I had.

" That was about the Blackwater Dam. Now, there was a bit in the book about stealing hens . . ."

Mrs. Mackay had been ironing clothes on the kitchen table, but now she looked up fiercely.

" Twelve Black Minorcas they were," she said, " and the finest hens in Glencoe."

" Ay, ay," said Dan peaceably. " Just so. Just so. Now, as I was saying . . ."

" Twelve Black Minorcas," said Mrs. Mackay,

close on thirty years disappearing in a sentence and the old wound itching again, " and all we ever got was the feathers. Oh, fine we knew the navvies ! "

" They were decent enough chaps, but awful thirsty," said Dan. " They were allowed beer at the camp ; but beer was no use to them. It was the hard stuff they were after. They used to climb over the back glen there, down to Kingshouse Inn, and get fou. And then they would try to get back over the glen again, in the dark, and the bog, and the snow. I used to go up with the pony in the spring, when the snow melted. I've brought down as many as twenty. Poor devils. You'd see maybe a boot or an arm sticking out of a drift, and then dig. You can still see the graves up beside the dam. Half of them have no names over them. No one knew their names. You know, I was up on the hill last year, a wee bit off my usual road, and I came on a skeleton. Ay. Thirty year it had been there. There was moss on the bones and a bottle in its hand."

We stayed silent for a while.

" Twelve Black Minorcas," said Mrs. Mackay, and was interrupted by a thunderous knocking at the door. " See who that is, Dan." She returned to her ironing.

A gust of cold air whistled round the kitchen, blowing a grey fluff of wood-ash up the chimney. A voice at the door bellowed :

" Well, well, well ! Mr. Mackay ! And how are you ? Great ! Absolutely great ! We were . . . eh . . . we were just wondering if you could maybe be moving the ponies along a bit in the barn."

Mrs. Mackay sniffed. " Hamish," she said.

Instantly the kitchen was an uproar of barking

dogs, stamping boots, and voices still pitched to carry through the Glencoe gale. Chairs were pushed back. The room was suddenly crowded, and Mrs. Mackay, a maternal look hiding itself unsuccessfully behind a grim expression and a strident voice, was pushing two tattered figures up to the fire.

" Grown men like you, out on a night like this ! " she chanted, obviously not meaning a word of it. " You ought to be ashamed of yourselves. And soaked to the skin ! Eh, these climbers, always wet clothes and dirty boots ! Do you not think shame of yourselves ? "

Hamish evidently did not. He stood before the fire, grinning broadly and chuckling at each fresh remark. When the torrent had somewhat abated he introduced his friend, a strong, broad-shouldered lad called Jock Nimlin. Mrs. Mackay smiled.

" Sit you down," she said. " You'll be wanting tea."

II

Hamish and Jock had arrived near Glencoe on the previous day and camped at a place called Coupall Bridge, a spot so boggy and exposed that now, eight o'clock and black night, they had decided the barn was their one hope of refuge. Could they sleep in it ; and, if they could, would I help them with their gear ? It was not far to go—just a little way down the road—and it would be a very great help if I would only, as Hamish put it, do a Good King Wenceslas.

The night is talked of still. In Glasgow, one Monday in September is set aside as a public holiday ; and in the long week-end so provided it is the habit of

most campers and hikers to have their last fling of the
summer. This was the Saturday night of the 1934
Autumn Holiday, a night when hundreds were on the
roads and a sou'wester came roaring in over the Atlantic
and flung itself across Scotland in a flurry of rain and
hail. It poured into the western end of Glencoe, burst
through the bottle-neck at the east end, and went
bellowing, a thousand feet above the sea and stiff as a
stone wall, across Alltnafeidh on its way to the Moor of
Rannoch. We travelled with it. It sent us half-
running, half-stumbling along the road to Coupall
Bridge. There was no moon ; and mist, out of sight
in the rain and darkness overhead, cut out even the
starlight. It was an evil night.

"The boys'll be having a time of it ! " shouted
Jock.

"The boys ? " I said.

"Ay. The Creag Dhu. I'm in the Ptarmigan
Club, but I climb a lot with the Creag Dhu." He was
shouting almost into my ear. "One of them has a
two-ton lorry. He's taking twenty of them up to Fort
William on it."

"Is it enclosed ? "

"What ? "

"Is it enclosed—covered in ? "

"No. Och, the boys aren't fussy."

As we plodded on, I pictured twenty sodden
wretches clinging to the back of a lorry bucketing
along Loch Lomondside, and shuddered at the thought.
It seemed they were due at the barn at two in the
morning, and Jock, if they stopped and had room for
him, was joining them. But soon we had other things
to think about. A pin-point of light wavering in the

darkness ahead grew until it became an electric torch held by a sodden gentleman in an oilskin cape under which a rucksack gave him the air of a half-drowned hunchback. Behind him a dozen wet smears resolved themselves into ten men and two girls. We, too, had a torch. We stood and took stock of each other, like scouting parties come suddenly face to face in No Man's Land, which was more or less what we were, for this was no holiday resort, but the middle of a howling desert of a peat bog eighty miles from home.

" Who are you ? " asked the man with the cape.

" Ptarmigans," said Jock, " and this is Big Hamish of the Tricouni."

" Good. We're Lomonds."

" Who ? " I asked Hamish.

" Lomonds. Lomond Mountaineering Club. Johnnie Harvey's crowd. They work the Trossachs road, usually."

We leaned our backs against the wind and went into conference on the accommodation problem. The Lomonds, heading for the farthest north point to which any motorist could be induced to take them, had found themselves at Bridge of Orchy early in the afternoon, liftless, wet, and destitute. They had started to walk and since then had covered over a dozen miles, sheltering when they could and walking when they could not. They had had cover below a bridge at one stage of the proceedings, welcome because it was the first they had struck for over an hour ; but a Highland bull had had the same idea, and driven them forth once more. They were a bedraggled crew.

" Why not take the end compartment of Dan's barn ? " asked Jock.

" The end compartment ? The place where they hang the new deerskins ? Kinda bloody, isn't it ? What about Downie's ? "

" If it's Downie of Laggangarbh you mean," I said, " there's no room.   There's ten in his barn already."

" Goad ! Then it's us for the skins.   Ach, but you get used to the smell anyway.   So long, mate.   See you there."

The darkness swallowed them inside a few yards. We turned towards Coupall Bridge, around which that night was a morass of liquid peat.   We slipped and slithered along a track which petered out on a cliff of mud at the bottom of which was a narrow shelf and a tent.   Beyond the shelf was a river, invisible in the darkness, but, by its turbulent roar, evidently in high spate.   The wind came in great claps, so that the solitary tree beside the camp shrank screaming from it, and we felt so acutely a sense of space and lack of protection that we might have been sailing through a midnight storm in an open boat.

The tent, when we struck it, seemed alive.   When the guy-ropes were detached from their pegs, the wind which tore at the canvas sent them lashing like whips through the air, each with its wooden guy at the tip. We lost skin and temper.   A good twenty minutes were spent in subduing clammy canvas and cramming errant jerseys into rucksacks by the light of a single torch, during which time we were muddied to the roots of our hair and nearly fell into the river.   At last we climbed the mud cliff and regained the road.

Only then did we appreciate the full force of the wind, for it was in our faces, and Hamish's " little way down the road " had turned out to be every inch of three miles. Bent almost double and weighed down by wet equipment, we tried to beat our way back to the barn. Towering upwards on our left was the rock bulk of Buachaille Etive Mor, the Great Shepherd of Etive, finest peak in the district and one of the half-dozen finest in Scotland. Behind was the Moor of Rannoch, bare, desolate and houseless for thirty miles. At our right hand was one of General Wade's more improbable roads, untouched and forgotten for a hundred and fifty years, winding in desperate zig-zags up into the mountains. And ahead was Glencoe, grimmest pass in Scotland, where the cliffs beetle almost over the road: Glencoe of the massacre, the new road, amateur photographers, and orange peel. But we saw none of these things, for we could not raise our eyes into the stinging rain, and would have seen nothing if we had. The night was black, and filled with the noise of wind and roaring stags. Soaked, we reached the barn and stumbled inside.

III

When Glencoe was bought by the National Trust, and posterity assured that petrol pumps should not blossom in the gorge nor desirable bijou residences break out upon the slopes of Bidian nam Bian, Dan Mackay retired from the business of deer-stalking on an estate where deer were no longer shot, and went, after forty years at Alltnafeidh, to live at Bridge of Coe at the bottom of the Glen. Since then his house and barn have been in other hands, and I know nothing of the existing state of affairs there. But in the early nineteen-thirties Dan Mackay's barn was a rather more versatile institution than its appearance might have suggested. It was a simple, single-storeyed building of concrete and corrugated iron, lacking both the romantic appearance and complicated system of draughts which distinguish most Highland barns. It had had a predecessor ; but, as it had stood in the path of the new road, the men who built the road's concrete bridges and culverts built a concrete barn to compensate for the loss of the old one. Thanks to its position, it rapidly became a howff for all sorts of people.

The Glencoe road has always been a main trade route to the south, for it is the one reasonable gap in the barrier of mountain and bog which stretches otherwise unbroken from Rannoch to the sea. That way came the cattle drovers, heading for the southern markets : that way went the Redcoats when there was trouble in the North. A constant though dilute stream of traffic has passed through the Glen from time immemorial. For the rich there were inns, Kingshouse at the head of the Glen and Clachaig at the foot ; and for the man with a few shillings in his pocket these two inns are still there. But for the cattlemen and other unmoneyed creatures there were barns and out-houses or perhaps a bed in a crofter's cottage.

With changing times the flow of cattle ceased ; but there were still tramps to fill such barns as the one swallowed by the new road ; and with the new road came new traffic and new tramps. The concrete barn became hotel to the Creag Dhu, those of a like persuasion, and such patrons of the former barn as still tramped the roads. For penniless mountaineers it was an ideal spot : some of the finest climbing in Britain

1 The cave on Ben Narnain. Left to right: 'Tough Bloke', 'Jewish Harp Expert', Jimmy Glover, Hamish Hamilton, Alastair Borthwick, Jim Wood, Bill Small and A. N. Other (back to the camera).

2 (above) Sandy had enough energy to pose for this picture during the 'Hunger March'. The position is near the 'Bad Step' with Lochs Scavaig and Coruisk in the background.

3 (right) John Boyd on Spur Climb, Sgurr an Fheadain, a few days after the 'March'.

4 (opposite page) Coire Lagan idyll – with two regular members of the team, Margaret 'Midge' Stewart and Alec Small. c.1933

5 Hamish Hamilton in Glen Brittle, 1935.

6 (top right) One of our better winter days – on Ben Lawers, above the clouds with William Makins on the left.

7 (right) Midge Stewart and Alastair Borthwick in Corrie Lagan, 1935.
Photo: Arthur Bullough

8   Chorus line at Glen Brittle, 1933 – Borthwick and Small (wearing tea cosy) on the right.

9   (left) 'Midge' in action on Ben Cruachan.   10   (right) Jim Borthwick, the author's brother, on the Cioch Upper Buttress, 1937.

11 12 (above and right) Stob Gabhar
before and after the ice climb. The couloir
is the slot running to the summit. The
small photo shows Midge and Hamish . . .
'Midge's hair was still rattling'.

13   Hamish Hamilton belaying 'Hugh' Knowles up Pitch 9 of the Chasm,
Buachaille Etive Mor, during our prolonged ascent in 1935.
This and all other photos: Borthwick collection

was on its doorstep. For the professional tramp it was equally convenient : it was a milestone on the regular tramps' route which heads south over Rannoch Moor and turns due east at Auch Farm for Glen Lyon and, eventually, Tayside. At that time there were only two places between Clachaig and Glen Lyon where a tramp might expect to find a roof over his head, and Dan's barn was one of them.

So it was that on this night of gale and driving rain we were not alone in our choice of shelter. By contrast with the darkness outside, the three candles burning on the floor seemed unbearably bright ; and, as the draught from the open door sent shadows careering round the walls, several seconds passed before we could distinguish those who had arrived before us. In the background were the two ponies, filling two of the three horse-stalls. Disposed over the floor and the remaining stall were seven people.

There were two motor-cyclists who had borne with the rain as long as they could and then decided that anything would be better than going on. There was a small and very moist tramp with whiskers like a cairn terrier ; and a tall tinker with a bicycle, a case of needles and thread, oilcloth, and other cheap odds and ends for sale to farmers' wives. He was brown as a berry, wiry, and, excepting only Jock at Blairgowrie, the only mink I ever met who talked too much. It seemed he had quarrelled with the rest of his clan and was working as a freelance. I was surprised to see him, for tinkers seldom sleep in barns. They prefer their tents in any weather.

There were two lads from Glasgow who had intended camping, but had decided against it when the weather broke ; and the seventh was a middle-aged, stout man, with white hair, a red moon-face, and a bicycle. He was decently dressed, and did not look like a flattie. Nor did he appear to be a farmer, or any other type of person except a tradesman of some sort, though the number of tradesmen of any sort to be found in barns in Glencoe on dirty nights in September is very small indeed. I found later that he was an itinerant french polisher, probably the only one of his kind in Scotland. His name was Walter.

So much for the barn proper. At one end an extra compartment had been tacked on to it, and from the rafters of this annexe depended a collection of deerskins, newly hung and stinking to high heaven. From the annexe came sounds of song and mouth-organs : the Lomonds were bedded in.

We pumped up our stove, cooked supper, and listened to the tinker telling a lurid tale of a fight he had once taken part in at Blairgowrie. But it was too lurid to be true ; and most of us, I think, preferred to listen to the weather instead. It was as wild a night as I remember. The wind howled and raved, each fresh burst of rain hurling itself against the tin roof with the rip of tearing calico. We spread straw on the concrete floor, crawled into our sleeping-bags, newspapers, old sacks, or whatever we carried by way of bedding, and prepared to talk the night away. It was then 10.30.

The stories started in earnest. By continuous snubbing, we contrived to silence the tinker, who wanted to tell us about another fight he had won. We were growing a little tired of his fights. He always won.

Then the flattie with the cairn terrier whiskers bestirred himself ; and, amid a great rustling of newspapers and with much sniffing, told how he had once found a dead badger near Oban and tried to convert it into hard cash, badgers being practically legal tender in the circles within which he moved. For some reason he had entrusted the beast to another tramp . . . "He wass Irish, and ass mean ass plazes" . . . to take it to a taxidermist.

"He came pack and told me that he had cot nothing for it, nothing at aal, and he had thrown it in the harbour," he said in the slow, halting manner of one who talks in English and thinks in Gaelic, " Putt when he cot trunk that night I wass suspeecious. And I went to the taxidermist And I wass told that he had peen paid twelf shillings for it. Yess, to make sporrans with. And when I cot pack, the Irishman wass cone, and I haf not seen him since, the tirty tog ! "

That was all the story. It was not a very good one. But then it seemed to have the elements of great tragedy, for we had before us the man to whom it was real and important, the tramp, so small and simple, with his whiskers jutting like a bramble thicket, and his red nose, and his pale eyes, and his unspeakable boots, sitting in the horse-stall and grieving for his twelve shillings. He had lost them four years before, but the incident rankled still. He had probably not held twelve shillings in one piece since. He did not look a very efficient tramp.

"Talking of dirty tricks," said Jock Nimlin, " did you ever hear the story Dan Mackay tells about the Jew pedlar and the Blondin ? "

And, having assured himself that the story was fresh, and his audience that it was a shocking affair, he set the stage. The Blondin had flourished in the days when the Blackwater Dam was being built, and was simply an endless cable, slung from high pylons, which bridged the four miles between Kinlochleven and the Dam. From it were suspended huge buckets which carried most of the food and equipment to the navvies' camp. To the Kinlochleven end of this contrivance had come a small and ill-favoured Hebrew, peddling pins and buttons.

" The Kinlochleven navvies told the man he'd do a roaring trade up at the camp, and that the easiest way to get there was to climb into one of the Blondin buckets. It was about ten to five at the time, and the only thing they didn't tell him was that the Blondin stopped for the night at five o'clock. The poor wee devil spent the night with the fear of death on him, slung in a bucket between heaven and earth a mile above Kinlochleven. They were a wild lot ! "

A burst of rain rattled on the roof, and the ponies shifted uneasily in their stalls. The audience's attention wandered until the squall died, then focussed again as Jock continued.

" And there was the fellow that kept six lodgers in a hut under the Blondin, a mile below the Dam," he said. " Fed his lodgers with a pole, he did. It was a big pole, long enough to reach the buckets as they went by. This bloke used to go out and hunt for a soft spot under the Blondin, and wait for a bucket with food in it, and then reach up with the pole and release the catch that held it upright. Out would fall all the grub on to the heather."

One of the motor-cyclists interrupted. " But why wasn't he caught ? " he asked.

" Because he took good care no one saw him, and

because the catch could have been released anywhere in four miles. He fed six hungry men for six months without spending a penny on grub ; and they never got him in the end. He did a moonlight flitting the night before the police arrived."

Hamish was impressed. " Great ! " he said, openly admiring. " Deserved to get on, that lad. Bet he's running an hotel now."

Jock grunted, and talk became general. The tinker slipped in another fight before anyone could stop him, and one of the motor-cyclists told of a brakeless journey through the night. Jock mentioned one summer and autumn when he had set off with three friends to climb mountains and beat grouse on alternate days. They abstained from shaving and grew beards, " a beard," said Jock, " being a thing you could stick a comb in and run a hundred yards without it falling out. We all passed the test. The beards scared the grouse fine. Ay, ay. And there was the night after the toffs had shot all the grouse they wanted, and some of the boys were in the marquee having a drink from the left-overs, and one of the guests came in, and he had a drink with them, and they found he'd never heard " The Ball of Kirriemuir " sung, and they carried him home at midnight. Ay, yon was a holiday right enough."

There was silence for a little, as is the way on these occasions, while we searched our memories for stories. It was Walter the french polisher who spoke first. Walter, a slow well-padded soul, had lost his job five years before, and ever since had been going round the country on his bicycle, visiting what he called Big Houses during the day, and sleeping at night in barns and such-like howffs. At the big houses he found enough french polishing to keep himself alive. He carried all he owned on his bicycle.

One night Walter had slept in a gasworks. It was cold and wet, and the engineer on night duty had let him in and allowed him to sleep near the furnaces for warmth. So, as he had the engineer's permission to be there, Walter was annoyed when a police sergeant flashed a torch into his face at midnight and demanded to be told his name.

"Now, what I think of the polis is nobody's business," said Walter, "but when a polisman asks your name, there's only one thing to do, and that's give it. So I says : ' Walter So-and-so.'

"' Hum ! ' says he. ' Walter So-and-so. And where d'you come from, Walter ? '

"Now, I knew I was in the right, me having the engineer's permission ; but just the same you've aye to be careful with the polis. So I tells him I'm on the road.

"' Hum ! ' says he, ' Exactly. And what might be your age, Walter ? '

"Mind you, I'm having a job keeping control of myself, but I tells him my age. Then he starts asking about my family, and I as near as anything tells him to go to blazes. But the polis is the polis, so I tells him about my family. After that he asks me a lot of other questions, and I answers them, though all the time I'm wondering what he's getting at.

"Then he slaps his notebook shut and scowls something awful, and I was sure I was finishing the night in the clink, and me with the engineer's permission, too ; and I was just starting to tell him about the engineer when he starts to howl and laugh.

" ' I'm afraid I don't see the joke,' I says, stiff-like.

" ' Ho,' says the sergeant. ' D'ye no' ken what night it is, Walter ? '

" ' No,' says I.

" ' This is the night we take the census,' he roars, and walks out."

To this day Walter does not see anything funny in this story. He told it, not as a joke, but as an example of the iniquity of the police. He was a man with a grievance. This, said his round red face, was the sort of trouble which befell honest french polishers in search of a doss, this the type of indignity inflicted upon earnest seekers of permission from engineers. Such things were not laughing matters. He became quite huffy when we chuckled.

The candles were burning low, and the singing had ceased in the malodorous compartment next door. Stories, somehow, did not come so easily to mind as they had done earlier in the evening. The tinker, baulked of his own tales of prowess, had been asleep for half an hour, and the motor-cyclists were nodding. Even the gale had a restful sound.

" How about it ? " asked Hamish. " Lights out ? "

For reply, Jock threw his boots at the candles. A little teasing out of hay, a slight adjustment of bones to bare concrete, and we slept until cheers and curses announced the arrival of the Creag Dhu on their lorry. Jock picked his way across the crowded floor to the door.

" So long," he whispered.

" So long," we replied, and slept again as the lorry with its tempestuous cargo disappeared into Glencoe.

CHAPTER NINE

SHILLING A NIGHT

THE Scottish Youth Hostels Association, a society administered by its own members and designed to build as many hostels as possible in the Scottish country side, was formed in 1932. I did not hear of it until the following year ; but since then I have been a member, a privilege which has cost me—the sum has varied with my age—between three and five shillings a year. The number of hostels has grown slowly ; but to-day my membership card entitles me to walk into any of sixty-odd hostels scattered up and down the more remote parts of the country, and there obtain a bed and blankets to sleep in, a kitchen and pots to cook in, and a commonroom to play, talk, sing, and argue in, all for the charge of one shilling a night.

Being interested in such matters, I am biassed in their favour ; but, even when trying to think of them in a detached way, I cannot rid myself of the conviction that the youth hostel movement is one of the more important social innovations of this century. It has opened up thousands of Scotland's deserted square miles ; but that is relatively unimportant. What is important is that the Association numbers its members by the tens of thousands, and that the vast majority of these people have so little money that they could not, without the help of the hostels, spend their week-ends in the country and in the fresh air. What was once not even within reach of a summer holiday has become a week-end playground.

Throughout that year when I first learned of hitch-hikers and caves, barns and bird-watchers, the Youth Hostels formed a solid core of experience. These other things were aspects of the truth that a new week-end society was growing up ; but they were off-shoots and perversions of the central fact that the hostels were the basis of the movement. During that year I slept in many hostels, meeting there doctors and bank clerks, barbers and typists, students and labourers, office boys, grocers, insurance agents, shop assistants, engineers. There appeared to be no class of society to which the appeal of the hostels did not extend ; and so they were, and, to my mind, still are, the greatest library of ideas and human experience in Scotland.

I argued about the three-colour process in films with a cinema projector salesman in Glen Clova two years before the process reached the screen and the public knew anything of it, about the relative merits of Rangers and Third Lanark in Arrochar Hostel, about the poetry of Chesterton at Langholm in the Borders with two Edinburgh journalists. I was preached the Douglas Credit System at Inverbeg on Loch Lomond by a budding chartered accountant, and modern methods of road construction by a surveyor at Ledard Hostel on Loch Ard. I learned Boer folk songs from two South Africans in Glen Nevis ; and at Arrochar, early in the year, four German girls taught me the most exquisite volkslied I know.

That was a night. We had all been caught in a downpour of rain which had started early in the afternoon and grown progressively worse ever since. By early evening, sixty drowned rats were crammed into Arrochar Hostel commonroom, with more arriving off the hills every few minutes. It was a big room with unvarnished pine walls, solidly built tables and benches, and, at one end, two kitchen sinks, shelves of pots and pans, and a vast array of pigeon-holes where each person kept his or her food. In the centre of the room was a huge cast-iron stove ; and above it, stretching from wall to wall, was a rope laden with a sodden, steaming, and fantastically mixed collection of garments. They were the clothes of most of the sixty.

We were all decently clad ; but some had had a struggle to preserve an air of respectability. I, having been washed out of the Cobbler corrie and being blessed with a leaky rucksack, was wearing a kilt and a scarlet bathing costume ; John, making the most he could of blanket and a pyjama jacket, had a bed-ridden look about him ; and William, swathed entirely in brown blankets, looked like a cross between a Roman senator and a Franciscan friar. He appeared to favour the former part, for he was striding about declaiming the more popular sayings of M. Antony as reported by Mr. Shakespeare. And everywhere were people in coarse shirts and jerseys, short trousers, kilts, breeches, frying their sausages and ham, and making tea on the stove.

When we had fed, we were at that replete stage of tiredness when conversation lapses and the tendency is to stare at the stove and dream. Then a curious thing happened.

A lad with fair hair and a very brown face was sitting on the floor near the stove with his back to the wall ; and he started to play a mouth-organ very quietly to himself. No one paid much attention. Then he played a tune I had not heard before ; and I noticed he was staring over his mouth-organ at a girl who was writing letters on the other side of the commonroom. And another thing I noticed was that, although she was obviously too busy to notice that a tune was being played, she was beating time with her foot.

The mouth-organist frowned and started the tune again, a little louder this time ; and when he had played it half through the girl sat up with a jerk, stared at him for a moment, and then gave him such a smile as would have made a misogynist delirious. After which, she sang.

The lad must have discovered that she was German, for it was a German folk-song he had played ; and she, hearing without hearing, had not realised immediately that the song, in Scotland, was unusual.

Now she sang, clearly, beautifully . . . " Wenn komm, wenn i komm, wenn i weider, weider komm . . ."

". . . weider, weider komm . . ." chimed in three other German girls who were with her, and the bumble of conversation in the commonroom hesitated and died. People turned round. Dirty dishes were left dirty.

". . . . weider, weider komm kehr ich ein mein Schatz bei Dir . . ."

Song is so common in the hostels that it seldom interrupts the business of the day. One goes on with one's job, singing but not pausing. But this was different. The girl was beautiful, and sang like a lark ; and so intense was the silence that the mouth-organist, who normally would have been blasting to make himself heard over the din of singing and small-talk, was playing softly and well. I felt as if I were not breathing. She held those sixty people, cyclists, hikers, all sorts, to the last note ; and then the cheering must have been heard half-way up the Cobbler. It was an extraordinary business.

They made her sing it three times, and gradually caught a few of the words . . . " Wenn i komm, wenn i komm " . . . that was easy ! " Weider, weider komm," sang the girl. " Weider, weider komm," bellowed the mob, enchanted by the thought that they were singing in German. They stamped their feet and roared at the rafters. It was a great success. " Wenn i komm . . . ! " Marvellous !

That started it. Would we—she smiled again— sing some Scottish songs, please ? Would we ! And there was, too, a lad with a good tenor voice, the Gaelic, and a chest like a barrel. We sang all night. We sang " Die Lorelei " and " Banks o' Loch Lomond," " Stille Nacht " and " An t' Eilean Muillach," " The Cockle-Gatherers," " Die Wacht am Rhein," " Deutschland Uber Alles " and " The Eriskay Love Lilt."

Hot faces yelled by the stove. No one heard the mouth-organist, swamped now by the crowd drawn in from distant draught boards and games of whist. The atmosphere was thick, a compost of cooking, bodies, and steaming clothes ; but no one cared. Every one sang, so that dripping travellers arrived at the door and were amazed. Sixty people, far gone in song, can make a great deal of noise.

We were still writing out the words for each other at lights out that night ; and I still have a post-card headed " Swabisches Volkslied " with the words of that first song scribbled on it in a curious spidery handwriting.

Next morning everyone had gone.

CHAPTER TEN

ICE

FOR the maximum and minimum of pleasure in the open air, winter mountaineering in Scotland is pre-eminent. There are days when the sun shines in a thin, wintery-blue sky, when the snow under one's boots is like crisp toast, when the icicles and ice cornices are shot with cold blues and greens against the silver of the snow-fields, and blue shadows lie behind the drifts. Then it is good to be above the snow-line, breathing the brittle air and gazing a hundred miles across a sea of peaks from Nevis or the ice-draped cliffs of Bidean.

These days when the air is sparkling-clear are a snare and a delusion. They are interspersed by other days—oh, how many other days !—when the world is grey, ten yards across, and possessed of a raging wind which numbs fingers and toes joint by joint and plasters the mountaineer with ice until he creaks like an armoured knight ; when the thought of hot baths is too poignant to be borne, and food and bed fair trade for one's immortal soul.

Yet such is the peculiar constitution of man that winter mountaineering is a disease both infectious and chronic. There are two reasons why this should be so. First, man is an optimist : yesterday was filthy, but to-morrow the sun may shine. In just such a manner must the tiger, its appetite for human blood whetted by some luscious Hindu maiden, content itself with many a skinny patriarch before more attractive fare again comes its way. And second, the reasoning powers of man are obscured by an inability to distinguish between things he enjoys doing, and things he enjoys having done. Sitting by the fireside, dry, fed, and rested, he thinks of the struggle he had on the mountain, the elemental pitting of his strength and skill against blind nature, the Valkyrie music that was the wind, and the fact that he—he, John Smith, clerk, blackcoated pen-pusher—by dint of cunning, strength, and a compass outwitted the forces arrayed against him.

" By Jove ! " says John Smith.   " It was magnificent ! "

Of course, on the mountain he had not eaten for ten hours, had not felt his feet for three, had been soaked to the skin and then frozen solid, and for half the day had wished heartily that he were dead. But he does not think of these things. John Smith is warm again.

This may explain why Hamish, Midge, and I left Bridge of Orchy at seven o'clock one February morning to climb Stob Ghabhar, ignoring both the rising wind and the combination of red dawn and grey-purple clouds which meant snow before the day was much older. Robin drove the car. He was not feeling too fit, and meant to leave us high on the mountain before the difficult climbing began. It was a cold, grey morning ; and by the time we had parked the car at the tiny tin schoolhouse beyond Forest Lodge and struck uphill, snow was falling and it was evident that we might expect no improvement in the weather.

Not the least of Stob Ghabhar's peculiarities is its pronunciation, which is " Gower " ; but this excites little comment in a country where Mhadaidh is pronounced " Vaatee " and the mountaineering tongue trips lightly over such morsels as Sgurr a' Ghreadaidh, Beinn a' Chaoruinn, and Bidein Druim nan Ramh. It is a misleading mountain. Seen as the motorist on the Glencoe road sees it, across Loch Tulla, it is a gentle peak, well-proportioned, and without difficulty. There is no hint, from that angle, of the fine corrie which cuts into the north face of the mountain and hides itself there. We were making for this corrie. Somewhere in it, we knew, was the celebrated Upper Couloir of Stob Ghabhar, a narrow slot splitting a cliff for three hundred feet and reputed to be filled with ice. It finishes on the summit, 3,500 feet above sea-level.

By lack of judgment we chose a bad route, so that it was not until one o'clock in the afternoon that we said good-bye to Robin and began to traverse across a slope of steep, soft snow towards the foot of the couloir. The snow was thigh-deep, more was falling, and the whole slope was so unstable that we should have been distressed but not surprised to see it all peel off and go sliding 1,500 feet to the corrie like a rug on a polished floor. Nobody was saying very much. Even Midge, who had been known to conduct a discussion on architecture while leading a rock-climb, was silent. It was a cold and subdued company which gathered at the foot of the couloir and peered upwards into the dark cleft above.

Midge and I smoked while Hamish went prospecting, but it was an unsatisfactory business. The cold was so intense that we could remove neither our leather over-mittens nor our gloves ; and, as holding a cigarette in the equivalent of an iced boxing glove is difficult, we soon threw away the wet and disintegrating stubs and fell to flapping warmth back into our hands. We were well wrapped up. We both wore wind-proof jackets and breeches, thick stockings, puttees, and boots, and many layers of underclothes. I had the usual balaclava helmet, a bizarre but comforting garment which covers one in wool from the crown of the head to the shoulders, and has a little window cut in front for the eyes and nose ; but Midge had lost her balaclava and was making do with an ancient and lengthy scarf, which she had wrapped three times round her head after the fashion of one who is assailed by toothache. The ends were lashed round her neck. We were a lovely couple.

A face framed by a frozen balaclava peered over the edge of a boulder above us :

" Come on ! Next for shaving, please ! "

Midge, tied midway on a hundred-foot rope, assaulted the boulder, which blocked the entrance to the couloir. When she had succeeded in joining Hamish on top of it, I followed on and found them standing in steps cut in forty-five-degree snow. What I saw beyond them I did not like.

The Upper Couloir of Stob Ghabhar is an objectionable part of the world which in summer is shunned by all right-thinking mountaineers, and resembles an immensely deep and long corridor running uphill at so steep an angle that a hand stretched straight out from the shoulder will touch the floor ahead. The couloir is roughly twelve feet wide, fifty feet deep, and three hundred feet long.

In these dimensions it is no more notable than scores of other gullies in Scotland ; but the feature to which it owes its fame is a slab of rock which interrupts its bed. This slab is a hundred feet high, and occupies the middle third of the couloir. Its angle is steeper than that which lies above and below—for approximately eighty-five feet the angle is sixty degrees, and the top fifteen feet are vertical—and it is decorated by a cascade of water and an abundance of slimy vegetation. As the walls which rise on either side of this depressing piece of work are almost impossibly steep, and as the only way to the top lies up the middle of the watercourse, no climber has been known, in summer, to do more than raise his hat politely and climb back down the couloir. But in winter, thanks to the altitude of the couloir, all of which lies above the 3,000-foot contour, the watercourse freezes for months on end, acquiring layer after layer of ice—thick, solid, honest ice in which steps may be cut. Also, the ascent in a normal season is made easier by drift snow, which frequently gathers in this convenient slot to such an enormous depth that it wipes out most of the slab and leaves only the top ten feet projecting above the surface.

It was on this drift snow that we had been depending; but now Hamish was standing, unenthusiastic for once in his life, with a sour expression on his face. The snow was only a few feet deep. The ice pitch was still a hundred feet high.

"Know any songs, you two?" asked Hamish, facing the ice and swinging his axe.

We said we did.

"Well, sing. I've an idea you're going to be here for a long time."

So saying, he addressed himself to the ice. Soon the splinters were tinkling past us, hopping over

the lip of the big boulder, and disappearing silently into
the void.

II

It was not a nice day. The wind, now risen to
gale force, was howling up the rock and ice funnel in
which we were perched, bringing with it the curse of
winter climbing, which is snow-spume. Snow-spume
is millions of hard, frozen-snow nodules, in size,
consistency, and appearance similar to those sharp
pellets of sugar with which some bakers are wont to
decorate their biscuits. I have not known these
objects draw blood when backed by a gale ; but they
are painful and supernaturally penetrative. They
seek out one's underwear, and there swoon ecstatically
back into their original liquid state. They come as
the sands of the desert, smoothing all before them, and
covering one's boots to the ankles as steadily and
visibly as those same sands fall in an hour-glass.

The cold was intense, and I was far from happy.
To take a photograph (which in the end was out of
focus, moved, and under-exposed) I had removed my
mitts and gloves for a period of time which I am certain
did not exceed two minutes. That had been half an
hour before, and I still had no feeling in three fingers.
As I had been reading a great deal too much about the
Himalayas, I was convinced that I was frost-bitten and
doomed to spend my future life (at the moment a
somewhat nebulous prospect) with only seven fingers.

" It's all right, pet," said Midge. " I'll knit you
special gloves."

Her position was parlous in the extreme. I, being

at the tail of the party, had the choice of all the steps
between the boulder and the ice, and had chosen two
which were sheltered from above by a projecting angle of
rock. Midge had no such protection, but was standing
in two steps in the centre of the couloir, exposed to
anything which might fall from aloft, where Hamish
was hewing great chunks of ice from the fall as if his
life depended on it, which it did. These pieces of ice,
some of them weighing a pound or more, were no longer
tinkling : they were beginning to hum. And Midge was
stopping most of them, a circumstance which she was
doing her best to ignore.

At this stage of the proceedings she was singing
" From Greenland's Icy Mountains," and keeping her
hands warm by beating them, in time to the hymn, on
the seat of her navy-blue climbing breeches.

" Come on, you, sing ! " she shouted to me. I was
demoralised. " If you start feeling sorry for yourself,
you're sunk. You'll die. You'll get frost-bite and
your hands'll drop off. Come on, sing ! "

" I've got frost-bite already," I said. " Let me
die in peace."

Hoots of laughter and a well-aimed chunk of ice
came from above. I laughed too. We finished
" Greenland's Icy Mountains " and weighed into
" Rock of Ages," with Midge singing the bass part and
myself the soprano, because my knowledge of harmony
was zero. Not that it mattered. Half of it was lost
in the gale.

After two hours Hamish was eighty feet up and
approaching the vertical ice which capped the fall ;
I could feel my fingers again ; and we had sung all the
hymns and all the Gilbert and Sullivan we knew. It

was then that Midge hit on a song which for some insane reason we always afterwards associated with difficult places and reserved for moments upon mountains when all was not as it should be. Why this should be so, I do not know. It was a daft institution, like a family joke. But somehow, in the Stob Ghabhar couloir in a gale, was born the convention that in moments of adversity Midge should sing "Minnie the Moocher."

Now, the peculiar merit of "Minnie the Moocher" is that it is a song which can only properly be sung by two or more people. It is a low ditty with many verses, each of them culminating in "Hi-de-hi-de-hi," screamed by the verse-singer. Whereupon all others there assembled reply "Hi-de-hi-de-hi," and wait for the next line, which is "Ho-de-ho-de-ho" and calls for a similar reply. There is a good deal more in this vein, and then the final line is reached and bawled by everyone simultaneously. It is, simply, "But Minnie had a heart as big as a whale."

This song is not edifying, but it is warming. We sang it to the last line of the last verse—"She was a good girl, but they done her wrong"—sent a final volley of hi-de-hi's into the teeth of the gale, and felt much the better of it. But it was the peak of our efforts, and we failed to reclimb it. We were tired, and cold. The gale, having blown all the snow-spume on the mountain up the couloir, changed its mind and blew it all back down again. Midge was still slapping the seat of her breeches; but now, where her gloves struck the cloth, two navy-blue patches showed up sharply against surroundings grey with ice. A thin film covered us from head to foot. The singing faded,

and died. The wind had its own way. Midge made
only one effort at a revival, and even then the joke was
no joke, because it was true.

"Hey!" she yelled.

"What?"

"Hey! I've been wondering what was rattling."

"Well, what was it?"

"It's my hair."

III

We watched Hamish in silence, apathetically, as a
tired man may stare almost unseeingly from a window
at crowds of strangers going about business which is
no concern of his. We had stood in the same steps,
with the wind blowing sixty miles an hour and the
temperature near zero, for more than two hours, and
had long since ceased to take any keen personal interest
in what was going on. Nothing was quite real.
Intense cold has a strange numbing effect on the brain
as well as the body, and both reach the limit of their
endurance before very long. Thereafter, those parts
of the brain which register pain and fear hibernate.
A body is cold and miserable; but it is not, somehow,
quite one's own body. A brain registers a set of
circumstances which should induce panic; but the
brain has retired into a protective casing, from which
the circumstances glance off, leaving no mark. He
who is cold lives in a passionless and almost painless
world. That is why death by exposure must be,
contrary to popular opinion, one of the more pleasant
routes to Paradise.

The ninety feet of rope linking Hamish to us was stiff and iced, so that three or four feet of it could have stood upright in our hands like the Indian rope trick in miniature. Hamish was neither cold nor in a trance, as we were. He was hot with exertion ; and his brain was keyed up to solving the most difficult ice problem he had ever been called upon to tackle. Below him was the zig-zag staircase he had carved in the sixty-degree ice, where he had stood upright in his steps, balancing with confidence, and swinging his axe with both hands : but now the ice was vertical, and he was no longer in balance. He was cutting " letter-box " handholds, to which he clung with one hand while he cut with the other. Nor did ordinary foot-holds now suffice. So steep was the ice that he had to chip out long, shallow slots which would allow his whole leg from toe to knee to fit into the slope. Midge and I, staring upwards like philosophic cod, decided that he could not possibly hold himself in balance long enough to finish the job.

In this we were wrong, though many unorthodox expedients were to be adopted before the time came, after Hamish had been nearly three hours on the wall, for Midge to follow. Hamish was inspired. His agility and timing were beautiful to watch. The ice-fragments were falling less frequently now, for he was tiring ; but he was wasting no energy. He was cutting rhythmically ; and when he moved, it was smoothly, slowly, inch by inch, like mercury rising in a thermometer. And then we saw that he was heading for a tiny recess in the ice where it might be possible for him to stand on his feet once more and relax his strained arms. He balanced up over a bulging mantelpiece of green ice, hesitated, and stood up. He could rest.

A fragment of a shout came to us through the gale,
now blowing upwards once more.

" What ? " we yelled.

". . . axe . . . axe . . . send me up an axe."

Midge had untied long since, and, though I had
moved up beside her, only a few feet of rope were left
in my hands. I loosened the rope from my waist, and
tied on the end of it the lighter of our two axes, which
was Midge's. Moving cautiously, for he was far from
secure, Hamish pulled it up, detached it, threw down
the end of the rope, and jammed the shaft of the axe
into a crack he had found in the ice.

After passing the rope once round the axe, he
climbed upwards, evidently hoping that the axe would
hold him if he fell. As it happened, the rope had
frozen to such a stiffness that it would not slide round
the shaft of the axe, and he had to gather a few feet of
slack to allow him to climb farther. Still, it was a
psychological safeguard for the critical seven feet which
lay between the recess and the lip of the fall. Physically,
it was no safe-guard at all. If he had slipped, the axe
would not have held for a second. When he had passed
the difficulty, we flicked the rope free.

With a sigh of relief we saw his boots disappear
from sight. He was up. Or so we thought. We tied
our spare hundred-foot rope to the one which by now
was fully extended, and waited for the signal to start.

It did not come. Minutes passed, and still the
second rope crept slowly upwards, until, half an hour
after he had passed from our sight, and two hours and
three-quarters after he had first stepped on to the ice,
Midge and I were standing beside each other, looking
puzzled, and staring at the end of the rope, which

Midge grasped in her hand. We had been shouting for five minutes, and had heard nothing. The gale had cut us off. We did not know whether Hamish was on easy ground or difficult, whether our hold on the rope was inconveniencing him only slightly, or halting him on a vertical wall from which it would ultimately drag him. One thing only we knew, and that with utter conviction : we had to cling to that end of rope like grim death, for it was our sole link with the outer world, and we had only one axe between two.

Midge tied on, took my axe, and started. As the slack above her was taken in as she advanced, we presumed that Hamish was secure. In due course she crawled over the lip and disappeared. It occurred to me suddenly that I was very lonely.

IV

I passed the time by tapping out tunes on the knees of my breeches, which, having been soaked by wet snow low on the mountain, had frozen solid. The cold was by now having its full effect. Eyebrows and eyelashes had frozen up, a beard of icicles hung from my balaclava where my breath condensed on the woollen chin-piece, and nothing seemed to matter very much any more. There was a certain academic interest to be gained from speculating on the method Hamish would adopt to lower the rope and axe back down to me, and I had sufficient wit left to keep an eye on the ice-lip for signs of them ; but his was a problem which did not seem to have any direct bearing on my future comfort. I felt I should just stand there for ever, watching the lip and admiring the view.

Only a little of the view could be seen : most of it had to be inferred. The air was heavy with mist and snow, so that on three sides either rock walls or ice shaded off into greyness above. The fourth side, behind and below me, was greyness alone ; but I knew it hid a 1,500-foot drop to the floor of the corrie. I wished that Hamish would hurry.

I thought I heard a metallic sound from above, but no axe appeared. This must have been Hamish's first attempt to lower it. He and Midge were ensconced a hundred feet above the lip, at the top of a gentle slope of ice down which they were trying to slide the axe ; but the drag of the frozen rope was too great, and the axe refused to slide. Meanwhile they were becoming colder and colder, and less and less patient, and eventually were reduced to the desperate expedient of tying the axe to the rope, coiling up a hundred feet of slack, and heaving the lot outwards into space. The last they saw of the axe was when it disappeared over the lip, going hard, and dragging the second hundred feet of rope after it. In just such a way do tough gentlemen in the Arctic harpoon whales.

The whale is not a very vivacious creature at the best of times, and is said to look upon the world with a jaundiced but nevertheless peaceful eye. Even in moments of stress, as when a harpoon is planted in its flank, it exhibits peevishness rather than royal rage, for the dominions of its body are so vast and scattered that messages travel slowly from them on their way to its brain and are modified in the passing. In the couloir I thought I understood whales. I felt I should get on well with one. And when the harpoon hove in sight, travelling at that rate of thirty-two feet per second, at which gravity has ordained such unimpeded bodies shall fall, I was no more distressed than the whale must be when it sees an insignificant ship and ignores the gun mounted upon its prow.

The axe struck the lip, and, as it bounced, the knot became untied. The axe left the rope, and came down in one clear sweep of a hundred feet, touching nothing.

As the couloir was barely twelve feet wide, with myself placed neatly and vulnerably in the centre; as an ice-axe is a heavy instrument decorated with a six-inch steel pick at the head and a heavy spike at the end of the shaft; and as, even if the axe should not impale me, there was nothing to prevent it sailing 1,500 feet hopelessly beyond my reach, there was cause for some alarm on my part. But, as I have explained, the whale outlook prevailed. I watched the axe in its flight as an over-worked astronomer may observe a minor and unimportant meteorite. Even when its shaft stabbed two feet into the frozen snow and its flight was miraculously arrested within reach of my hand, nothing worthy of comment appeared to me to have occurred. I wanted an axe. There was an axe. I picked it up.

The rope dribbled down the ice and came to rest a few feet above me. I climbed to it and tied myself on. And so, five hours after we entered the couloir, we met on the summit of Stob Ghabhar. I remember being particularly taken by the icicles on Hamish's moustache.

v

The mountaineering novice, in the course of that

research through text-books which is one of the early
symptoms of the disease, frequently comes upon a
statement which puzzles him. It is to the effect that,
on a big climb, a leader shall be appointed who shall
decide all matters of policy which may arise during the
day. This may or may not be the man who actually
goes first on the rope. Beginners have been known to
consider this sheer affectation, an attempt to make the
climb seem more important an undertaking than it
actually is ; and they may well climb for several years
before its full wisdom is impressed upon them.

Then they appreciate that the human male or
female, when tired and miserable, is ripe for mutiny,
can give a mule points in stubbornness, and contracts
diverse and bigoted notions on such matters as routes
to be followed and directions to be taken. Tempers
become frayed ; and, as was once the case on the
summit of Ben Ime when I and fourteen others wanted
to depart to fifteen different points of the compass in
order to reach home, there is a tendency for the party
to burst asunder and lose itself. The appointment of a
leader early in the day mitigates these evils, and offers
some guarantee that the one member of the party who
is right and actually reaches home will not have to
spend the night scouring the country-side for the others.
And if the leader should be wrong, it is better to be lost
in company.

It is one thing, however, to possess wisdom, and
another to apply it. Though we had read the text-books,
Hamish, Midge, and I belonged to that school of
thought known in political circles as rugged
individualism. And we were lost, though even on that
point we were not agreed. The road which straggles

up the glen from Forest Lodge is a primitive affair which has made no great mark on the landscape. It is little better than a track. While we had been on the mountain much snow had fallen, and a doubt had arisen in our minds as to whether or not we had crossed the road without knowing we had done so. Furthermore, the night was now pitch dark, and we had no torch. If, as Midge and I held, the snow had wiped out the road and we had crossed it, we were now heading for the outer bog where we should assuredly spend the night. If, on the other hand, Hamish's theory were sound, we had not yet reached the road and any retracing of our steps would only take us back to the top of Stob Ghabhar.

We had a map and ten matches, six of which were wasted before we were convinced that, in the absence of shelter from the wind, the map could not be read. By sheer force of invective, Hamish was induced to follow us through a succession of snow-covered peat hags, into most of which we fell, and, eventually, to a burn. Here we found a sheltered bank and struck one of the matches. Before it died, we had opened the map at the proper section, and Hamish had consulted his compass.

"Now," said Midge, "we've only three matches left. We'll have to do this to a system. Hamish, you take the top third of the map. Alastair, you take the middle. And I'll take the bottom. Are you ready?"

We said we were ready. I struck the first match against the box, broke the head off it, and failed to find it again in the darkness. There was an awkward sort of silence.

"Nice weather we've been having lately," said

Hamish gently. "Warm for the time of year, don't you think? Here! Gimme those matches!"

The next match burned down to his fingers while we each scanned our section of the map. He struck the last match, and again there was silence while we memorised what we could. The match flickered out.

"We aren't on my section," said Midge.

"Nor mine," said Hamish.

"I think we're on mine," I said. "It looked to me as if we were on a burn flowing west to Tulla."

"Fine!" said Midge.

"Fine my foot!" said Hamish. "My compass says this burn is flowing east."

Despondency settled over the party once more; but eventually it was decided that the burn might, in its meanderings, have doubled back on its course for a short distance before heading west-wards once more. We decided to follow it, but not before Midge and I had made a fruitless excursion back in the supposed direction of the road.

There followed a purgatorial half-hour of floundering through peat and heather, with the burn bending now this way, now that, and the thought always at the back of our minds that we were hours overdue and that Robin must by now be a very worried man. If we had been certain that we were heading for the car it would not have been so bad; but our doubts were so rapidly being replaced by the certainty that we were walking away from it that, after yet another committee meeting, we agreed to turn back if we did not find the road within ten minutes.

Five minutes later a mysterious red light appeared on the far side of the burn, by now a young river. We stopped. The light moved. We shouted, and sighed with relief when we heard Robin, querulous now that anxiety was relieved, demanding to know where we had been. He had searched for us so long and diligently that his electric torch was almost exhausted, and was no more than glowing. Also, he felt that mismanagement was implied by the fact that we had the rucksack containing all the food, which we had been too cold to eat ; whereas he had the rucksack containing all the spare clothing, which he had no reason to wear. We waded knee-deep through the burn, and joined him. It was eight o'clock. Fifty yards away was the car.

Two hours later as we motored home, fed and warm once more and with the old rosy film creeping between us and reality, Hamish finished the song he was singing, stretched himself luxuriously, and sighed.

" Gosh ! " he said, with an enthusiasm normally attained only by American radio commentators. " What a day ! Great ! Ab-sol-utely great ! "

CHAPTER ELEVEN

PEAT

DOUGIE and I were sitting outside our tent on the fringe of the Moor of Rannoch. It was a night of black and silver, with a full moon sailing over the mountains and shedding a track of light across the loch to our feet. The night was still, and threw into sharp relief the small sounds which floated to us over the loch, and the crackles and explosions of the fire we had made from the ruins of a rotten birch ; and when the fire died in a bed of glowing ash the small sounds came into their own, so that we could hear, for our ears were stretched to hear them, every flicker of the wings of the solitary bat flipping back and forth overhead, and the distant roar of a stag. The scraps of a meal were scattered around us. We were fed and replete. Wood smoke was sharp in our nostrils. The Milky Way arched over us. It was a night to dream about.

" We shall go," said Dougie, " by the north shore of Loch Laidon, and then through the gap between Loch Laidon and Loch Ba. And pray heaven we can ford the Abhain Ba."

The afternoon train had dropped us at Rannoch, now four miles behind us ; and next day we meant to cross the Moor of Rannoch, though why we should have wanted to cross it I am hard put to it to explain, unless it was that we had been reading *Kidnapped* and fancied ourselves as Alan Breck and Davie Balfour. Many trivial factors contributed to our desire, no single one

of which would have been sufficient to send us out into
the bog, but whose cumulative appeal could not be
resisted. The Moor was, for instance, the biggest
desert in Britain, four hundred square miles of houseless,
roadless peat. Then again, none of our friends had
crossed more than its northern fringe from Rannoch to
Kingshouse, where there was a track of sorts ; and we
knew of no one who, in recent years, had crossed the
heart of the bog. We could obtain no advice about
routes, and had to work out our own from first principles
and a map.

This alone might have been sufficient to set us off ;
but, in addition, week-end after week-end we had gone
climbing in Glencoe, and, crossing a corner of the Moor
on our way north, had seen the enormous dun-coloured
swamp stretching twenty miles to Rannoch, fretted
by lochs, peppered with boulders, and magnetic in its
vastness and solitude. It had grown on us ; and the
growth had been by no means retarded by the queer
tales Day Mackay had told us about it from time to
time. By these varied stages had our tent come to
the shores of Loch Laidon, and ourselves to be lying
beside it before the fire, stuffed with herring, oatcakes,
tea, and honey.

We spread out our map and considered it in the
firelight. The journey appeared to be divided into
three stages, of which the second seemed the most
difficult. Here, beside Loch Laidon, we were on firm
ground. From the distant edge of the Moor, which we
hoped to reach by the following night, a rib of high
ground which was presumably also solid ran a few miles
into the bog. But between Loch Laidon and the rib
was low-lying ill-drained peat and a fat little river which

would have to be forded somehow. Once over this
middle section, we decided, we should find no difficulty.

But it was too wonderful a night to waste on maps.
We returned to our contemplation of the moon and the
mountains until the glow faded from the fire and we
could lie no longer. It was September, and cold. We
crawled into our sleeping-bags. The last thing I
remember hearing was the distant stag, sick for love,
belling to the moon.

II

The tendency for walkers and climbers to admire
the view is always most marked in the early hours of the
day. There are base creatures who insinuate that the
object of such halts is not the view at all, but a desire for
rest ; and in fairness to this theory it must be admitted
that stops become infrequent after the party has
warmed to its task or sees the end in sight, whereas
early in the morning its members are collectively and
individually struck by the beauty of the landscape and
are forced to admire or photograph it at intervals of
ten minutes. If a day ever comes when all hikers and
mountaineers are fighting fit, the manufacturers of film
will feel the draught.

So entranced were Dougie and I by the panorama
unfolded to our gaze by the mere flicking aside of the
tent door, that it seemed to us sheer sacrilege, bad
taste, and a casting away of the gifts of providence to
arise from our beds before nine o'clock in the morning,
though we had wakened at eight. It was a perfect day.
The morning mist was rising like steam from the surface
of Loch Laidon ; and in the bracken tangle before us a

thousand spiders' webs were spread like lace,
dew-covered and glittering in the sun. A branch of
scarlet rowan berries overhung the tent door ; and the
sky, crisp blue above, shaded by imperceptible degrees of
grey down to the smoky mountains on the horizon.
Such were the blandishments of bed, loch, mountains,
moor, sausages, and honey that ten o'clock had come
and gone before we had the tent stowed away and the
first mile put behind us.

According to the map, we were still on the
Rannoch-Kingshouse track and were to remain on it
until we struck south at the head of Loch Laidon and
embarked on the second stage of our journey ; but peat
bogs have a way with tracks. I am not prepared to
say that one does not exist : if the officers of His
Majesty's Ordnance Survey say there is a track, far be
it from me to contradict them. All I wish to record is
that three miles west of Rannoch Station the path
therefrom, so far as we were concerned, dived into the
bog and there perished ; and that so uniformly dull was
the waste of hummocks, tussocks, and patches of rock
which followed that I am now reduced to the device
invented and nobly exploited by Hilaire Belloc in
The Path to Rome.

As you may remember, in the course of his journey
Mr. Belloc came on occasion to stretches of country so
drab that neither wit nor ingenuity could make them
bearable in print ; and on these occasions he simply
ignored the countryside and said : " I shall now tell you
a story." And behold, when the story was over he had
skipped thirty miles. So to cover the gap between our
belated start and the moment when we discovered that
Rannoch Moor was a much more interesting place than

we had bargained for, I propose to go one better than
Mr. Belloc, and tell two stories.

The first is short and grim, a moral tale for those
who persist in cross-country walking without a compass
in their pockets, and concerns those Children of the
Dead End already mentioned in this book. The tale
is told up and down the Highlands, and if it is not true
it deserves to be. It seems that when the Blackwater
Dam was being built, back in 1905, large numbers of
navvies wandered north in search of work ; and those
who had a little money travelled by what was then the
quickest route. They left the train at Rannoch
Station, as we did, and set off to cross Rannoch Moor.

Now, as will readily be understood of a camp where
so little was known of its inhabitants that names were
sometimes not forthcoming for their tombstones, it
frequently happened that it was no one's business to
see that these wanderers arrived in safety. No one
knew they had started. They were not expected.
Under these conditions, many navvies crossed the
Moor.

But there came a day when a navvy at the camp
was expecting a friend, and the friend did not arrive.
Perhaps the man forgot about it : perhaps he let things
slide for a day or two. In any case, after a week had
gone by, there was still no friend, and it was remembered
that dense mist had been lying over the Moor for days.
A search party was gathered, and set out.

They found the friend all right. He was dead.
But the point of the story is that while they were
searching for him they found six human skeletons.

The second story is more cheerful, and deals with
daftness on a major scale, and with the railway which

brought us to Rannoch.   The railway crosses the fringe of the Moor, and so villainous was the ground upon which it was built in 1889 that the engineers floated it across on brushwood rafts, in the same way as the engineers of the twentieth century floated the new Glencoe road across the opposite corner of the Moor on concrete rafts.   The whole railway, from Glasgow to Mallaig, was something of a feat ; and so it occurred to seven gentlemen who were concerned in the building and planning of it that it might be a good idea to follow the proposed route of the line throughout.   This was before work on the railway had started.

In due course they found that the only section they had not covered was the long loop over the Moor, and this they set out to do, ignoring, apparently, the fact that the month was January and the weather vile. This was only one of the facts they ignored : there were others equally cogent, as, for example, that most of the expedition's members were on the wrong side of forty, and that one of them was sixty, wore a felt hat, and carried an umbrella.   Their courage was commendable ; but the few plans they made suggest that they visualised the journey as the kind of walk one takes between church and lunch on Sunday mornings.

After a fearful voyage up Loch Treig in a gale and a rowing boat they struck out into the Moor, at that moment lightly decorated with sleet and so raked by wind and hail that progress was almost impossible. Yet, by some miracle, they crossed it, though how they contrived to do so is one of the unsolved mysteries of exploration.   Among the peat hags which the railway now crosses in a few minutes these unfortunate gentlemen wandered, utterly lost, for two days.

These two days were not uneventful. Inevitably, once the mist had come down and reduced visibility to a few score yards, they began to wander in circles. The results were dire. They fell into peat hags; they disputed vehemently about the route; they became exceedingly cold and wondered if they would ever again know the feeling of dry underwear; and they one and all agreed that if ever they crossed Rannoch Moor again it would be in a first-class railway carriage. Shortly after this decision had been reached, and they had, as they imagined, plumbed the coldest and dampest depths of misery, the elderly owner of the felt hat piled the unbearable upon the unbearable by relapsing quietly into unconsciousness and collapsing on the heather.

This left six professional gentlemen in a state of great alarm as well as discomfort, and the upshot of the conference which was immediately held round the recumbent sixty-year-old was that the party should divide into two equal parts, one to hold a species of wake round the victim, and the other to scatter itself upon the face of the Moor in an attempt to find help.

This was done. Three men disappeared into the mist and shortly lost touch with each other, while the remaining three prowled, in an attempt to keep warm, round and round the knoll where the elderly gentleman, rain streaming down his face, was laid out like a Viking chief slain in battle. Unfortunately, one knoll on the Moor of Rannoch is indistinguishable from any other knoll on the Moor of Rannoch; and presently the party discovered that it was circling an untenanted mound of peat, a mistake which, when it had been rectified, was insured against repetition by tying a handkerchief to the umbrella and planting it in a prominent position at the gentleman's head. Having, so to speak, put down a buoy to mark the wreck, they resumed their perambulations and continued them until help arrived.

Meanwhile, the others had been having heavy weather. Two lost themselves with such diligence that they had to be collected later by the search-party, leaving only one man to be the prop and stay of the expedition. This gentleman wandered for an unknown length of time and in the end was rewarded by a most heartening sight, a wire fence. This appears to have been too much for his nervous system, for, overcome by relief, he collapsed over the fence and there remained, either unconscious or asleep, for several hours. When he recovered, he followed the fence and in due course found a shepherd. A search-party was raised, and the whole expedition, including the umbrella and its owner, was brought to safety none the worse for its experience.

There is no moral to be drawn from this story, for the seven foolish virgins, empty cruses and all, came by no lasting hurt. Obviously, they were luckier than the navvies who were to follow them in later years, and had small cause to escape with their lives. In point of fact, if they had started twenty-four hours later they would have spent their second day in a blinding snowstorm and almost certainly have perished. Still, it was a notable crossing, and one, I feel, which might even yet be commemorated by the railway company in whose service all seven had been engaged. I like to think of a recumbent statue, placed beside the railway line mid-way across the Moor and carved from the porphyry of Glencoe, with a porphyry handkerchief and umbrella standing bravely at its head, and porphyry raindrops arrested for ever on its cheeks. Prowling round the plinth would be six gaunt figures, seeking shepherds. Only so, I feel, can justice be done to a great undertaking.

III

We are now at the point where the western shores of Loch Laidon strike into the heart of the Moor, and where one may say without fear of contradiction by His Majesty's Ordnance Survey or anyone else that there is no path of any sort or kind whatsoever. Ahead, the Moor stretched towards a distant fringe of mountains in waves of mottled brown, a tawny wilderness void of all signs of man's handiwork. It seemed to us drab and dead ; but soon we had our first hint that the Moor supported a life of its own.

The rock which underlies these miles of peat must be granite, for Loch Laidon is fringed, not by slimy peat walls as might be expected, but by little beaches of golden sand ; and these beaches were as greatly ploughed up as is that at Blackpool during Wakes Week. Here the inhabitants of the Moor had come to drink. Here, we could say, had come a stag ; and he had scratched his side with his antlers, because one of the points had scored the sand and left a mark. And these smaller prints were those of his hinds, following him to the water. And these, only slightly smaller, would be a fawn's. It was all written plainly there on the sand ; and as we followed the tracks the game took hold of us, so that we shouted to each other at each fresh discovery. The deer were not alone on the Moor. Grouse, said the sand, had been pottering about in a splay-footed way ; and we saw one set which must have been made by a fox, one of the big fellows who live in the hills and make the harried Lowland foxes seem pigmies. The claw-marks were stubby and not curved inwards, so we knew it could not have been a wild-cat.

It was strange, seeing all these things in a wilderness where there did not appear to be a single living thing within miles, though our reason should have told us that a desert so ringed about by sporting estates must inevitably have become a game sanctuary. At that stage we had seen no deer.

We came on them later, out in the middle of the Moor. We had become somewhat entangled in a system of peat-hags between Loch Laidon and Loch Ba, where the bog had split open like a well-baked cake, leaving in the peat great crevasses ten feet deep, with slippery walls and an evil-looking black scum on the bottom. The scum was of the consistency of porridge, and the ground round the hags swayed as we stood on it like a spring mattress. We were crossing one of these, using for foot-holds old tree roots which projected from the slime ; and as we clambered over the lip on the far side we saw a hundred deer go streaking across the Moor and up over a hillock on the skyline.

They were moving deer, deer at their best. The Stag-at-Bay-Monarch-of-the-Glen pictures with which the Victorian engravers plastered the parlours of the poor in taste remind me of those seedy, off-colour beasts one may see by the dozen in winter, grazing by the roadside, tame as cows, forced by the high snows into a fearlessness of man and a poor condition of body. I have seen them, just so, hundreds of times, the head up-flung to sniff a passing charabanc or the grain with which Dan Mackay used to hand-feed them. Then

their flanks were shaggy, dirty-brown, and lifeless, like
the wrong kind of cheap fur coat. But these deer were
different. They were sleek and magnificently red. The
languid stare and movements of the winter had gone :
they were alive. Each beast moved with the rhythm
and spring of a bouncing ball ; and the effect of the
herd seen in the mass was the smoothness of flowing
water, a liquid band of red undulating over the
inequalities of peat and heather. Suddenly the herd
wheeled and stared at us, stock still with the abruptness
of a cinema film stopped at a single frame ; and as
suddenly bounded again into flight. The Moor was
empty once more.

We lunched beside the Abhain Ba, the short but
sturdy river which flows from Ba to Laidon. Bread and
butter were produced, and honey. We became sticky.
The store in Dougie's honey-pot dwindled as he enlarged
upon its vitamin-content and excellence in the
treatment of burns. Dougie keeps bees, and, despite
the fact that he is so stung during the honey season that
he is seldom symmetrical, he rates their efforts very
highly indeed. According to him that day there was
practically nothing that honey could not do ; and, as
the food was absorbed into our beings and the sun
played pleasantly down, I was almost prepared to
believe him, for it was a drowsy day and acquiescence
was easy.

We propped our backs against a boulder, sighed
contentedly, and congratulated ourselves upon our
wisdom in delaying our journey until the month of
September. If we had crossed in July we could not
have lain at our ease, caring nothing but that the sun
shone and we were fed ; for in the days of summer,

before a touch of frost has come to add zest to the night air, the bog breeds a multitude of insects. Some of these are harmless and beautiful, like the thousands of dragonflies which haunt the trickles of water among the peat ; but many are ugly and obnoxious.

Chief of this latter class is the cleg. South of the Border the cleg becomes the horse-fly ; but this is just another example of the inability of the English, who prefer to call a peewit a plover and a whaup a curlew, to christen their birds and beasts with names which are expressive. A horse-fly sounds a docile, faithful sort of creature ; but cleg is compounded of all evil, a harsh sound, pitiless and sly.

This is as it should be, for the cleg is a foul thing. It sneaks up behind its victim, fastens itself on the back of his neck or other exposed area of his person (Heaven help the man who bathes on the Moor !), and there gorges itself on blood until it is too drunk to fly away. I know of few more revolting sights than a bloated and blissful cleg clinging to a hand or knee, and few less endearing habits than that of the cleg which, having pumped its victim softly and unawares, stings him as it leaves him. That has always been for me sure proof that the cleg is an obscene creature to be swatted on sight.

The Moor of Rannoch in summer breeds them by the million, stout clegs of supernatural physique and arrogance ; and though I do not believe the gentleman who once assured me they had bitten him through a thick tweed jacket, I warn anyone who may be thinking of crossing the Moor in the months of June, July, or August, that the cleg is a factor to be reckoned with.

We repacked the rucksacks and forded the Abhain

Ba, though not without difficulty, for, flowing as it does from a big loch, its lack of length bears no relation to its width or volume. The Abhain Ba is short and deep, and could not, I think, be crossed after heavy rain. We wasted half an hour in finding a ford, and even then were thigh-deep over a floor of slimy rock. Still, we were relieved to find even so uncomfortable a crossing, as any hitch at this stage would have forced us towards Kingshouse, twelve miles out of our way.

But still the way was not clear to the rib of high ground. Almost immediately we found ourselves in another maze of hags, a soft spot where the ground quaked and horrid little bubbles plopped up through the scum. There was no danger, however. The Moor lies in a basin of granite and is not deep. I am certain that if we had slipped in at any point we should have struck bottom within three feet. Time and again we came on the narrow slots of deer leading through what appeared to be bottomless quagmires ; and, if further assurance were needed, we had it in the centre of this maze, for we came on a stag's wallow in a place where no beast would have ventured if the ground had been unsafe.

For some time we had been puzzled by the presence, in some of the herds, of coal-black stags. Here was the explanation, a pool of black water lying at the bottom of a hag, from one side of which projected the roots of a dead and vanished tree. The root was polished smooth, and on the surface of the water floated many coarse red hairs.

Peat, for all its unprepossessing appearance, is sterile and could almost be used as an antiseptic, a fact which is apparently appreciated by the stags, for they seek out these bog-holes, roll and wallow, and scratch themselves on the old roots which are generally to be found there. In this way they rid themselves of vermin and parasites.

Generations of stags must have visited the hole we found, for the old root was polished like an ivory tusk. By it and other roots we climbed clear and struck firm ground again, thinking how different our journey would have been a thousand years before, when the ancient Caledonian forest covered the Moor and the bog had not risen up and swallowed it. Peat, as I have said, is sterile. The organisms which cause decay cannot live in it. So, although to-day not a tree grows on the Moor, the skeletons of the old forest lie preserved for ever beneath its surface. Only among the hags do they outcrop like white bones, to give support to hikers and a scratch to the backs of stags.

The ground became firmer. We turned away and made for the rib, which seemed to offer dry footing for the rest of the journey.

IV

We were on the rib, a thousand feet above the Moor, watching a storm boil up from the north. The sun was low on the horizon, for we had lingered by a tiny lochan we had found scooped out of the hillside a few hundred feet lower down, and should have lain longer if the clouds had not gathered over Glencoe. It had been a pleasant little lochan, covered with the water-lilies which blossom so unexpectedly and delicately in the coarsest of moors. But now we were high on the hill, which was a small relation, many times removed, of the great wall of mountains hemming in the Moor to the south and west.

Storm or no storm, we stood and gazed. To the north-east Loch Laidon ran back to the mountains where our journey had started. North-west was Glencoe; and at our feet Loch Ba, only a few miles long, yet possessed of a shore so folded in upon itself and so intricately slit by rocky arms and inlets that to follow it exactly would be a day's march. South and west were the mountains, Buachaille Etive Mor, Clachlet, Stob Ghabhar, Beinn Dothaidh, Beinn Achaladair, Beinn Chreachain, names clumsy in print but music on the tongue, mountains presenting a three-thousand-foot barrier between the world and the Moor which crawled, brown and rolling, mile after mile, at their feet.

The storm broke. Grey curtains of rain, bellying from the wind like galleon sails, trailed their hems across the Moor, snuffing out the mountains gently one by one. We turned and ran for it, over the Glencoe road and across the arm of moorland which lies beyond Loch Tulla. By eight-thirty we were dining at Inveroran Inn, twenty-five miles from Rannoch station.

CHAPTER TWELVE

THE CORKING OF KING'S CAVE

IN the Black Cuillin of Skye there is a peak called Am Basteir, which is Gaelic for The Executioner. From one side of it grows a thin leaf of rock one hundred feet high and shaped, according to one's taste in these matters, like a shark's fin or an executioner's axe. It is known as the Basteir Tooth.

Any climber who should make his way to the top of the Tooth by the highly sensational route evolved by a certain Mr. Naismith will find that his best means of descent is an equally intriguing route devised by a certain Mr. King. This route starts in the nick on the skyline where the Tooth joins the Basteir, and is known as King's Cave.

Of King's Cave the mountaineering guidebook says that no one measuring more than thirty-eight inches round the waist should attempt the descent, and, once the cave has been seen, the reason for this statement is readily appreciated, for if anyone of greater bulk ever managed to force his way into it he would probably have to stay there for life. It would be like trying to push a Bass cork into a medicine bottle, and, the impossible having been achieved, trying to pull it back out again.

The route's sole outward and visible sign of existence is a hole in the ground only just big enough to allow an adult male or female to squeeze through ; and, having entered it, the climber squirms forty feet vertically downwards in pitch darkness as if descending an ordinary household chimney. This dark tunnel is so tight that most people have to breathe out before they can move in it ; and it is, moreover, not entirely plumb throughout, but bores its way back and forth down through the rock like the path of an industrious but drunken worm. It ends on the floor of King's Cave proper, which is set half-way down the Tooth, and is followed by another descent which is generally done on a hitched rope ; but the whole climb from top to bottom, tunnel, cave, and rope descent, has in the course of time come to be called after King's Cave itself.

I once met a very red-faced gentleman from Huddersfield sitting at the top of the tunnel with most of his under-garments bulging out over the top of his trousers like a little kilt.

" Ever hear of Sisyphus ? " he asked.

I said that the dregs of my school career seemed to tell me he was the fellow who went to Hades and had to spend his time rolling uphill a boulder which always rolled back down again.

"That's him," said the red-faced climber. "The very man. Well, have you ever tried to climb *up* King's Cave with a rucksack balanced on your head ? "

II

My own encounter with King's Cave was moderately amusing. Three of us found the little slot on top of the Tooth where the tunnel begins ; and Midge, being built on a neater scale than the rest of the party, was sent down to explore. After ten minutes of hard breathing, forty feet of rope had disappeared and a shout from below announced that she had reached the bottom.

Alec tied himself on, and in the silence before he started, a voice from the underworld began to sing.

" I'll tell you the tale," sang the voice " of Minnie the Moocher."

" In the name of goodness," said Alec, "what's that ? "

" Private joke," I said, and explained that we used to sing it in tight corners. " This corner's literally tight, so I suppose that's why she's singing it."

Alec snorted and disappeared down the hole. Now, Alec is no singer ; and anyway, he was far too busy grunting. So Midge did the " Hi-de-hi's " from the bottom, and I did the " Ho-de-ho's " from the top in a most satisfactory manner for three full verses, all of which came floating up from the bowels of the earth through a haze of grunts from Alec. The fourth verse was just beginning when, suddenly, all sound ceased.

Alexander had corked the Cave. He had arrived at the narrowest part, and twelve stones of solid flesh lay between me and the song.

This state of affairs continued for several minutes, and all I could hear was Alec complaining bitterly that the guidebook was lying. He was not, he said, thirty-eight inches round the middle, never had been thirty-eight inches round the middle, and, by the grace of God, never would be thirty-eight inches round the middle. Yet he had stuck. It was, he said, such a complete stick that he doubted if he would ever see blue sky more : he was doomed to die in a drainpipe, embedded in the rock like a fossil. Gurgles of the most horrid kind followed this statement, and a forlorn scraping of nails on smooth walls. I asked him what was wrong.

"Wrong?" he shouted. "WRONG! It's this blessed shirt, that's what it is! Damn thing's worked up to my chest and jammed there. I can't move an inch, and my blasted stomach's bare and rubbing on the rock! What's wrong! Now, if I could only . . ."

The conversation tailed off into a crescendo of groans and staccato yelps as if some monstrous bear were hugging the life out of him. By this time I was committing the cardinal sin of ignoring the rope which it was my business to manage, partly because I imagined there was no need for it, and partly because I was helpless with laughter. Then things happened. Ten feet of rope shot from my hands, a loud crash and a wail resounded in the tunnel, and the last verse of "Minnie the Moocher" floated upwards. The cork had been drawn.

And then, very quietly, came a voice.

"I think . . . wait a tick . . . I *know* I have wrecked my breeks."

Alec is precisely thirty-three inches round the waist, and of the twenty or so verses of "Minnie" I heard barely four. The moral is obvious. One of the many merits of climbing is that it tends to rid one of fat, but King's Cave should not be chosen by those who stand in need of reducing. Nothing short of starvation will ever get them out again.

CHAPTER THIRTEEN

LARIG GHRU

SCOTLAND has two great passes which, relatively
small though they are, exercise as vivid a local
appeal as the giants of Europe and northern India.
They are the Corrieyairack, where Wade's old military
road climbs over the Monadhliadths from the Great
Glen to Speyside ; and the Larig Ghru, chief pass of the
Cairngorms. Both are long, and both fulfil the prime
function of a pass, which is that it should link, across
some desolate region, two centres of civilization. They
have become the pilgrim routes of those who like to
take their pleasures strenuously. By far the finer of
the two is the Larig Ghru.

At eight o'clock in the evening my brother dropped
me at Coylum Bridge, a few miles from Aviemore, and
promised to pick me up on the far side of the Cairngorms
on the following afternoon. I said good-bye, and
turned along a little track to the Rothiemurchus
Forest, where a signpost points a single arm labelled
" Braemar " as if it heralded a motor road instead of a
scratch on the bare bones of the earth without so much
as a house to grace it for more than twenty miles.

No road goes over the Larig Ghru. The mountains
which we now know as the Cairngorms were once a high,
level plateau covered with ice which, forming glaciers,
gradually carved out beds for itself in the rock as rivers
do to-day ; and when, in the fulness of time, the
glaciers melted, the plateau had been cut up into a

group of separate mountains. The Cairngorms cover a large area. Most of the glaciers could only carve glens which ran back a few miles into the mountains before disappearing ; but in the centre of the range they cut a way clear through, a deep V running for more than twenty miles through the heart of the old plateau.

Near one end to-day is Braemar, and near the other is Aviemore ; but, as the summit of the pass is 2,700 feet above the sea and blocked with snow throughout the winter, not even the indefatigable General Wade ever had the temerity to drive a road through it. It has been left for the pleasure of stalkers, hikers, and climbers.

I knew I should have enough daylight to see me to the top of the pass, for it was a fine night in July and in these latitudes the sun at that time of the year never sinks very far below the horizon. The going was pleasant, for the Rothiemurchus is a beautiful place, and is a real forest. It actually has trees in it. It is not, for example, like Lord MacDonald's deer forest in Skye, which, so far as I have seen, has no trees at all ; nor is it like any other of the skimpy woods or wastes of peat which are called deer forests simply because deer happen to be shot in them. The Rothiemurchus is a forest, dense and green, where thousands upon thousands of firs cling to the foothills of the Cairngorms so profusely and without plan that anyone straying from the Larig path might easily lose himself amongst them.

My way climbed gradually upwards through the trees, which opened out every now and then into a clearing with sometimes a deer or two standing there

watching me ; and the farther I climbed the more did
the path twist and squirm as it avoided hummocks
where heather had grown over ancient roots and fallen
trunks.

And then the trees thinned out, and I emerged on
to a species of natural midden right in the mouth of the
Larig. The old glaciers had picked up all sorts of odds
and ends on their way down to the plains—boulders,
and mud, and rocks of all sizes and in vast quantities—
because glaciers flow like rivers and when they reach
low levels they melt, dumping all the solids they have
collected on their way. These rubbish dumps, or
morains, are common all over the Highlands, and there
is a particularly fine example where the Larig Ghru
begins and the Rothiemurchus stops. The mouth of
the pass is silted up with a great conglomeration of mud
and rock overgrown with heather. Into this soft stuff
a burn has cut its way, so that when I came out on to
the open hillside I found myself on the lip of a cutting
steep and deep out of all proportion to the tiny burn
which flowed at the bottom on the bare rock of the
mountains. So enormous was this accumulation of
silt that I had to walk nearly two miles uphill before
the bed of the burn rose to meet me and I too was
travelling on rock.

It was now past ten o'clock, and I was keeping my
eyes open for a convenient place to sleep, with a fairly
clear suspicion that no such place existed. The wind
had risen, which was awkward. Once an enthusiastic
half-gale finds its way into the funnel of the Larig, the
tentless traveller therein feels like a customer's change
coming down one of those suction tubes used in
department stores, for the wind is concentrated and,

once committed to the journey, has no option but to sweep over the summit and down the other side.

It seemed I had the choice of two evils. I could choose a sheltered bed among the masses of rock which had fallen from the cliffs on either side of the pass, thereby assuring myself of a windless but abominably uncomfortable night, for no grass or heather grows among the rocks there, and rock makes a hard bed. Or I could choose a good, soft, heathery place and be blown off the face of the earth. So I had to resort to guile.

I have found that in a confined funnel such as the Larig, the wind behaves like a car on a race-track or water in a river : when it comes to a bend, it tends to swing to the outside of it. This is a useful thing to know when one is carrying no tent and has to rely upon what the ground provides. The method is not entirely efficient ; but the chances are that an island of comparatively still air will be found on the left-hand bank of a left-hand bend, or the right-hand bank of a right-hand one, though the place may appear to be no more sheltered than any other part of the landscape.

So when I reached a point only a hundred feet or so below the crest of the pass and found that the track bore slightly to the left, I crossed to the left bank and dumped my rucksack. It did not appear to be at all a bad spot, though an annoying little current of air branched off the main stream and came sighing past from the direction of Aviemore. But that, I thought, could be baulked if I built a little dyke of stones at my head and lay with my feet to Braemar.

Stones were plentiful. The wall of the pass was steep, so that by climbing up a short distance and heaving down everything manageable within reach, a very fair collection had soon rolled down and come to rest beside the patch of grass where I intended sleeping. Then I built my dyke. I built it lovingly and with care. It was four feet long, three feet high, two feet thick, and the only dyke I ever built that stayed up for more than five minutes. I still like to think of that dyke. It was a masterpiece. I wasted an hour and all the knuckles of my left hand in making it, and my grunting would have been fearful if there had been anyone about to hear it other than two ptarmigan which watched operations from a nearby boulder, drawn, apparently, by the same form of hypnotism exercised in cities by pneumatic drills or men digging holes by any means whatsoever.

At last it was done. Ten minutes before midnight the two ptarmigan and I stood back in the half-light and admired my handiwork. And immediately the annoying little current of air branched off the main stream and came sighing past from the direction, not of Aviemore, but of Braemar. At this stage of the proceedings I had much wicked pride removed from my system, and eventually crawled into my sleeping-bag in a very bad temper indeed, for a boulder prevented my lying on the other side of the wall. The wind blew the wrong way all night.

I should like to digress here long enough to point out that, if the weather is at all reasonable, sleeping without a tent is ten times better fun than sleeping with one, provided only that you should not spend more than one night in the open. There is nothing extraordinary about it. The one is as comfortable as the other if the proper spot is picked. All that is needed is a lightweight sleeping-bag—preferably eiderdown, which is light and warm—and two lightweight groundsheets loosely stitched together down one side. You simply get into the bag and roll yourself in the groundsheets. Rain may mean damp feet ; but if only one night is spent in the open the bag can be dried at the end of the journey, and conditions are seldom bad enough to interfere with sleep. This is obviously not wild weather equipment, but it serves the pinch and has the merit of weighing less than three pounds.

And it is good to lie with your head projecting from one end of the cocoon—wear a balaclava helmet, by the way—with nothing between you and the stars, and all sorts of things going on around you which normally would never be noticed. Three deer went past me that night, walking very quietly, less than twenty yards away. That was after midnight, but it was still quite light. One of them disturbed a pebble, and I looked round, and there they were. They looked at me, but did not seem frightened. They moved slowly uphill until I lost sight of them.

There were other things, too. Even at that height, 2,700 feet up, there is plenty of life. Something set a stone rolling only half a dozen yards away, and to this day I do not know what did it. It was probably a ptarmigan, rooting about among the rocks, though what it was doing out and about at that time of night I do not know. I thought, too, that I heard a fox bark.

The wind roared by on the far side of the pass ; the cliffs above were black against the sky ; a little burn trickled past almost under my elbow. It was a grand night. I wrapped my scarf firmly round my seat (where, I find, it does most good : camp nights are cold), and slept.

III

At half-past nine on the following morning I met the first of the pilgrims. I was over the summit by that time and a good half-hour down the other side, just beyond the Pools of Dee, which are three or four brackish puddles near the top of the pass. I had been walking on rock and loose screes almost since I started, up and down through a landscape of boulders. The hikers, who were the first human beings I had seen for thirteen hours, were two lads from Edinburgh, and they had been walking since three o'clock in the morning. They had to reach home by evening, so they must have had a fairly crowded week-end : when I saw them they had covered about eleven miles from the road-end at the Linn o' Dee, and were roughly half-way to Aviemore.

After them came a steady stream. First were two lads on the far side of the burn, then three who had been on the way since six o'clock in the morning, then two from Corrour Bothy, a tiny hut dumped in the Larig itself and the only shelter within miles. By this time the Larig had widened from a notch in the skyline into a valley, and the trickle of water which seeped through the screes below the Pools of Dee was a young river. Beyond the river were the endless slabs and overhanging crags of the Devil's Point, a monstrous black mass of rock which fell over a thousand feet sheer to the level carse on the floor of the glen. Below it, looking absurdly lonely, was Corrour Bothy. I saw people moving about outside it, so I left the track where a cairn marks the ford, waded the river, and joined them.

The bothy is no more than a small shed with an earth floor and a leaky roof; but there were six people living in it, and two of them—Edinburgh lads again—had been there for a week, using it as their base for climbing and walking. I do not know how they manhandled all their food up to it, but they seemed quite happy. The situation was worth the effort, for the bothy was surrounded by four-thousand-foot tops—Ben MacDhui just across the way, and Braireach and Cairn Toul behind—with not a living soul in miles and miles. They said it was the most peaceful holiday they had ever spent.

We fell to talking, sitting on biscuit tins in the middle of the floor; and one of the lads said: " Do you know So-and-so? " and I said: " Yes. Do you know Whatisname? " And, as usually happens in these places, we found we had met most of each other's acquaintances and were not at all sure that we had not met each other too, years before. So we talked a little more; and a middle-aged man from Aberdeen sat in a corner puffing his pipe, listening but saying nothing.

After a while I said: " Any more word of the Great Grey Man? " to which the Edinburgh fellow said no, he had not heard anything lately, and did I think there was anything in that story. And I said I did not know, but it was a queer business just the same, and I should like to see the Great Grey Man myself.

Then the Aberdonian took his pipe out of his mouth long enough to ask who the Great Grey Man was. And we told him.

The Great Grey Man of Ben MacDhui, or Ferlas Mor as he is called in the Gaelic, is Scotland's

Abominable Snowman and the only mountain ghost I have heard of in this part of the world. He ranks high in the supernatural Debrett, for he has been seen by responsible people who have reputations to lose, most of them expert mountaineers accustomed to hills at night and not given to imagining things.

He first reached print about twenty years ago, when Dr. Norman Collie, a mountaineer of international repute who not only made first ascents of most of Scotland's major cliffs (a peak in the Cuillin is named after him), but climbed extensively in the Alps and was with Mummery on Nanga Parbat in the Himalaya, admitted that strange things had happened to him on Ben MacDhui. He had been alone on the summit at midnight ; and so peculiar were the things he saw there that he did not stop running until he was half-way down to the Rothiemurchus.

He related this experience at a dinner of the Cairngorm Club ; and immediately others, equally reputable, came forward and admitted that they, too, had seen queer things on MacDhui. According to their descriptions the Great Grey Man is a tremendous shadowy creature, and his height is variously reported to be anything from ten to forty feet. He appears generally at night ; and one's natural reaction is to run as fast as possible in the opposite direction.

There are two interesting points about the circumstances under which he has appeared. First, several men claim that they saw him before they knew of his existence : only when Dr. Collie gave the lead did they admit that they had seen something too, so they did not hear the tale and then imagine themselves into meeting Ferlas Mor. And second, there is no known mountain phenomenon which could account for him. If the sun is shining, it frequently happens that a climber's shadow is cast on a screen of mist some distance away, so that he can march along a ridge with a huge shadow stalking along in space beside him. But this is a common trick of mist and sun which would scare no one. I have seen it half a dozen times. It is interesting, but not in the least eerie. Anyone who makes a habit of climbing knows what causes it ; and, instead of running away, whoops with delight, rakes his rucksack for a camera, and tries to photograph it. It is known as the Brocken spectre, after the peak in the Hartz Mountains where it commonly occurs. But Brocken spectres cannot live without sunlight : the moon is not sufficiently bright. And the Great Grey Man walks at night.

I know two men who claim to have heard Ferlas Mor. The first was alone, heading over MacDhui for Corrour on a night when the snow had a hard, crisp crust through which his boots broke at every step. He reached the summit, and it was while he was descending the slopes which fall towards the Larig that he heard footsteps behind him, footsteps not in the rhythm of his own, but occurring only once for every three steps he took.

" I felt a queer, crinkly feeling on the back of my neck," he told me, " but I said to myself, ' This is silly. There must be a reason for it.' So I stopped, and the footsteps stopped, and I sat down and tried to reason it out. I could see nothing. There was a moon about somewhere, but the mist was fairly thick. The only thing I could make of it was that when my boots broke through the snow-crust they made some sort of echo.

But then every step should have echoed, and not just this regular one-in-three. I was scared stiff. I got up, and walked on, trying hard not to look behind me. I got down all right—the footsteps stopped a thousand feet above the Larig—and I didn't run. But, man, if anything had as much as said ' Boo ! ' behind me, I'd have been down to Corrour like a streak of lightning ! "

The second man's experience was roughly similar. He was on MacDhui, and alone. He heard footsteps. He was climbing in daylight, in summer ; but so dense was the mist that he was working by compass, and visibility was almost as poor as it would have been at night. The footsteps he heard were made by something or someone trudging up the fine screes which decorate the upper parts of the mountain, a thing not extraordinary in itself, though the steps were only a few yards behind him, but exceedingly odd when the mist suddenly cleared and he could see no living thing on the mountain, at that point devoid of cover of any kind.

" Did the steps follow yours exactly ? " I asked him.

" No," he said. " That was the funny thing. They didn't. They were regular all right ; but the queer thing was that they seemed to come once for every two and a half steps I took."

He thought it queerer still when I told him the other man's story. You see, he was long-legged and six feet tall, and the first man was only five-feet-seven !

Once I was out with a search-party on MacDhui ; and on the way down after an unsuccessful day I asked some of the gamekeepers and stalkers who were with us what they thought of it all. They worked on MacDhui,

so they should know.   Had they seen Ferlas Mor ? Did
he exist, or was it just a silly story ?

They looked at me for a few seconds, and then one
said :

" We do not talk about that."

IV

When we had finished this harangue, the Edinburgh
lad and I, the Aberdonian scratched his head and said :
" Well, I'm glad I didn't know about that last night,"
and then told us, quite casually, of the energetic time
he had been having. He had walked fourteen miles
from Braemar to the bothy on the previous night, and
had then been smitten by an urge to see the sunrise
from the top of Ben MacDhui, which is over 4,000 feet
high, the second highest mountain in Britain, and a
good three miles farther on.

He had reached the summit and so nearly frozen
on the way that at one stage he thought his fingers were
frost-bitten. Feeling rather sorry for himself he had
stamped round in circles, waiting for a dawn which
arrived, swathed in mist and completely invisible, at
4.15. In disgust he had returned to the bothy and
slept for two hours, a period which he apparently
deemed sufficient, for he left with me for the Linn o'
Dee.   There I waited for my brother, glad to stretch
my weary bones on a heather bank and let the world
go by ; but he, still restless, plodded onwards another
six miles to Braemar.   All told, he must have walked at
least thirty-five miles with a mountain thrown in, which
is more than enough for a young man, much less one in
middle life.   He finished fresh, too.

We met a dozen people with rucksacks before we reached the Linn. That was after we had signed the visitors' book at the bothy. It was the sixth visitors' book which had lain there ; and, like the other five, contained some famous names, even if the roof did leak and there was scarcely room to turn round. On the fly-leaf some wag announced that the telegraphic address was " Comfort, Cairngorms."

The Larig grew wider as mile succeeded mile, growing softer and more like the tourist's conception of the Highlands as the notch in the skyline fell behind, and in the end merging into Glen Derry, where the slopes are gentle and there are trees and the cottage of Luibeg stands by the river on the level strath. Outside the cottage, lying on the grass, were a neatly trimmed tree-trunk and several rounded stones taken from the river. Ian Grant of Luibeg is a great man at the Games with the caber, and he putts the weight like Ossian himself : here, evidently, he practised with no audience but the deer.

The track which had started high in the mountains as a few scratches on the rock had by now become a road of sorts, dusty and rutted, but still a road. The trickle from the Pools of Dee was a river, full-grown. Arguing with violence about diet and unemployment, two subjects about which I know practically nothing, the Aberdonian and I turned a bend and heard the cries of an ice-cream vendor and the voice of the internal combustion engine. We were at a Beauty Spot, a province of . picnic-land. The fringes of civilization were upon us.

CHAPTER FOURTEEN

THE CHASM

THE telephone rang.

"Hallo," said Hamish. "Hallo. Is that you, Alastair? Here, listen! It's been dry for ten days now."

"What has been dry?"

"The weather. No rain. Absolutely great!"

"Well?"

"What d'you mean, well? There hasn't been any rain for ten days. The Chasm, laddie, the Chasm!"

"Oh," I said, and began to think very quickly indeed. The Chasm was not a matter about which I cared to make up my mind on the spur of the moment. At that time, in May, 1936, it was causing a good deal of excitement among those who climbed. After a series of attempts extending over nearly forty years, a way had at last been found up it by a group of young Glasgow climbers during the drought in 1931; but it was only on the publication of the Scottish Mountaineering Club's *Guide to the Central Highlands* in 1934 that Hamish and many others first became aware that, cut into the side of Buachaille Etive Mor, which guards the entrance to Glencoe, was a gully difficult and immense beyond anything they had previously known.

Many were beginning to cast a speculative eye in its direction; but bad weather had prevented any attempts on it during the late spring. The function of a gully is precisely that of a drainpipe, and a mountaineer has as much chance of climbing the Chasm during a spell of bad weather as a fly has of crawling up the inside of a bath-pipe two seconds after the plug has been withdrawn. Ten dry days are generally conceded to be the safe prelude to an ascent by a party of experts.

" Look here, Hamish," I said. " The Chasm's a bit out of my class. But I tell you what I'll do. It's all wrong, and unethical, and all the rest of it. The Best People don't do it. But you get one other good man to join us, and I'll come like a shot. I'd sooner be a passenger with two experts than one. Get another man, and I'm prepared to risk it if you are."

All of which was highly improper. The climb was too much for me, and I should have refused. On a difficult route, no one has any right to regard himself as baggage. But Hamish was unconvinced.

" Och, don't be daft," he said.

" That's just what I won't be. The guide-book says there are two difficult traverses, and you know as well as I do that on a traverse the last man has to be as good as the leader. I want to be in the middle, and there isn't any middle unless you have three people."

" True, true," said Hamish sorrowfully. " I'll just have to dig up someone else. I'll 'phone you later."

That was on a Wednesday. On the Friday the weather was still brilliant ; and in the late afternoon he telephoned again.

" I've got the very man," he announced. " Met him last week-end on the Cobbler. Name of ——." He gave a name which, for the purposes of this story, shall be Hugh, " A great chap. A decent spud. Absolutely . . ."

" Yes," I said, " but can he climb ? "

" Can he climb ? He's been at it for years."

" Right," I said. " Count me in."

II

Buachaille Etive Mor, the Great Shepherd of Etive, has advantages of setting shared by few Scottish mountains. Ben Nevis, though its cliffs are magnificent, turns its back on the world and appears no more interesting than a pudding ; the Cairngorms, by reason of their vastness and number of peaks, appear from a distance flat and without character ; each of a score of other great mountains is cluttered up by outliers and lesser tops which either draw the eye from the main peak or hide it altogether ; but Buachaille Etive Mor stands alone, thrust forward from the end of a range, a gigantic cone of rock rising sheer and unhidden from the peat of Rannoch Moor. It is a mountain in its own right, rugged and yet shapely ; and if mountaineers ever had the task of selling Scotland it would be one of the last peaks to go.

The Chasm splits its southern face, starting among the upper rocks and falling almost to the road, a fifteen-hundred-foot rift cut deep into the rock. Many such gullies have sloping beds of scree, through which a few obdurate masses of rock, refusing to be worn away with the rest, poke their heads ; but there is no scree in the Chasm, nor does its bed slope any more than a staircase may be said to slope. Everything in it is either horizontal or vertical. It rises in fifteen gigantic steps connected by level, boulder-strewn rock ; and on either side its two walls rise sheer, it seems, to the sky. At the top is one final monstrous step called the Devil's Cauldron ; and the walls which enclose it—the bannisters, as it were—are only a few yards apart and over two hundred feet high. If Truth should ever wish to escape from her well, she will find her route simpler than the Devil's Cauldron.

We must have been excited, for we rose at the unprecedented hour of 5 a.m.; and if further proof of excitement be required, it is supplied by the fact that Hamish was excessively depressed. The sun was shining in a pale blue sky, clearing the night's frost from the heather; but Hamish was certain it would not shine for long. There would be rain, he said. The mist was rising, and fraying, and dissipating on Buachaille like frail curtains drawn one by one; but Hamish swore it would cling fast all day. The air was sharp and still. I felt I wanted to run until I was exhausted. But Hamish, moping in the tent, said it was cold and why on earth had he been fool enough to get up. Climbing was a mug's game, and if I called these things fried eggs he was Sindbad the Sailor. Would we please go away. All of which went to show that this was a Big Day, and that shortly, swinging to the opposite extreme of the pendulum and hallooing wildly, he would be clawing his way up impossible places, towing Hugh and myself after him like the tail of a kite.

I liked Hugh. He was a quiet soul, strongly built; and he did not fuss. He looked steady, though just how unshakeably steady he was to be before the day was out I had then no means of foreseeing. He went efficiently about the job of making breakfast and clearing up the tent, talking only when speech was necessary, and watching with mild astonishment my antics with camera and tripod as I tried to find the precise angle which would show Buachaille's morning mist to the best advantage.

By seven o'clock we had crossed a short stretch of moorland and entered the Chasm. It did not look very exciting. The walls were wide apart and barely twenty feet high. It looked exactly what it was, the bed of an almost dried-up stream ; and we did not even bother to rope before we scrambled, Hamish leading, up the little waterfall which confronted us. As his head rose over the lip of the fall, Hamish stopped.

"Gosh !" he said.

Two excited voices from below demanded to be told what he could see. But Hamish was in a trance.

"Gosh !" he breathed again. There was silence, broken only by the trickle of water which washed, unnoticed, over his boots. Then he moved, suddenly, explosively, depression cast off and forgotten in a moment. "Yippee !" he yelled with the full force of his lungs, heaving himself upwards and out of sight. Hugh and I looked at each other, listened to the clatter of his boots as he ran over boulders above, and scrambled after him as fast as we could go.

We found him, rapt, below the Chasm's first big pitch. At the point where we had scrambled up the waterfall the rock and heather outside the gully had started to rise steeply. The bed of the gully, however, did not follow it. The thirty yards or so which lay between the fall and the point where Hamish now stood were level, so that the farther we walked into the heart of the mountain, the higher did the walls on either side of us rise. But after thirty yards of this level progress it seemed as if the bed of the Chasm had suddenly yearned for contact with the outer world, for it shot skywards in two vertical steps of forty feet each, thereafter travelling horizontally once more before shooting upwards again and again in steps of varying heights. This process it continued to the point where, the final colossal step of the Devil's Cauldron apparently exhausting it, it merged peaceably into the summit rocks of the mountain.

But Hamish had seen only the first two steps and the ingenious method by which the mountain had built them. The walls, as I have pointed out, were wide apart ; but that was not sufficient to daunt the Chasm. It had produced from somewhere in its upper reaches two enormous boulders, each as big as a house and weighing thousands of tons ; and these, breaking loose and crashing down the gully, had jammed one above the other between the walls, one forty and the other eighty feet above the gully's bed. Using these as a book-end is used on a shelf, millions of smaller boulders had piled up behind them until they were level with the top of the step.

Frontal attack was hopeless, for there was a cave under each of the big boulders. Hamish paused only long enough to tie the rope around his waist before launching himself on to the right-hand wall and climbing until he had gained sufficient height to make possible a step across on to the top of the boulder. I, the passenger, followed. Hugh came up last. We had two hundred feet of rope.

Over the top of the second boulder poured a small but inquisitive stream of water, impinging upon the rock at a point where small holds made fast progress impossible. We climbed up the back of the cave almost to its roof, and then outwards along a little ledge until we could step on to the face of the boulder, maintaining the while that only malice on the part of the mountain

could have directed the stream of water to the precise
square foot of rock where the difficult step had to be
made. And so we came to the Red Slab.

The Chasm narrowed, so that we could touch both
sides at once. The sky was a blue slit, far above. The
way lay up a steeply tilted slab of red porphyry on the
left wall, unprepossessing, eighty feet high, and about
as secure as a piece of ripe camembert. All the holds
sloped outwards. Hugh and I crowded into a tiny
recess below the slab and waited for the avalanche.

" I'll try not to send anything down," said
Hamish.

Climbing of the most delicate sort must have been
necessary to limit the number of falling stones to the
half-dozen which did come clattering down the slab,
for the rotten, outward-sloping ledges were littered with
debris which required only the slightest touch to send it
bouncing and sliding about our ears. I sent down more
than a dozen when my turn came, while Hugh cowered
in the recess, hoping that no specially ambitious boulder,
leaping farther outwards than the others, would strike
the opposite wall and rebound on top of him. None
did ; and he had the satisfaction, once we were firmly
planted above him, of clearing away every loose stone
within reach on his way up, so making the slab a little
safer for future climbers. He came up slowly,
accompanied by bumps and crashes from below and
whoops of delight from aloft.

Hamish was in tremendous fettle. I think we all
were. There was something about the thin morning
air, the blue sky, the sun which was striking directly
into the gully, and the knowledge that we were
committed to a big climb, which had us keyed up

beyond our normal powers. I know I have never climbed better than I did that morning. Hugh, being behind me, I could not see ; but Hamish was flowing up places where normally he would have crawled an inch at a time.

Embedded somewhere in his memory were fragments of a song which was popular at that time, a nonsensical ditty called " No One Believes I'm a Mermaid," which in parts was reminiscent of " Die Lorelei." This he sang, ceaselessly and inaccurately, for the greater part of the day, relapsing every now and then into " Die Lorelei " for a few bars, and introducing a yodel or two for variety's sake whenever the mood took him.

" *Every hotel that I go to,*" he warbled, "*the manager says in alarm . . .*"

A loose stone whistled past us as he tested handholds far above.

" ' *. . . We're sorry that this should occur, but
We can't let a room to a turbot.' *"

" How's it going ? " we shouted.

" Dandy ! " came the voice from aloft." " ' *No one believes I'm a mermaid at all, but honest and truly I am, pom pom.' *"

The hours slipped by, and as they passed our confidence grew. Step succeeded step, each presenting a problem which Hamish solved in his stride. We began to feel at home in this rent in the rock where the narrowness of the sky, which greatly reduced the amount of reflected light, combined with the direct rays of the sun to make a world of bright highlights and dense, impenetrable shadows. Where the sun struck, the rock glared back at the eyes : where it did not strike was blackness. It was like living in a badly printed photograph.

Below the eighth step we halted and ate a second breakfast. All we had climbed so far had been accomplished in the eighteen-nineties by the early explorers ; but now we were faced by a pitch which resisted all attempts to scale it for several years and was said by one of the writers of that time to be utterly unclimbable. Like most of the " unclimbable " pitches of the eighteen-nineties it is not nearly so bad as it looks. It is called the Hundred-Foot for the good and sufficient reason that it is one hundred feet high. The way lies up a ragged scoop in the rock, and from top to bottom the scoop is only a few degrees off vertical.

This pitch illustrates better than any other I know the fallacious notions about rock-climbing which are held by the populace of this country. Guided solely by illustrated jokes in magazines, the uninstructed imagine that the rock-climber hauls himself upwards by his arms, scraping wildly with his feet the while ; whereas the truth of the matter is that he climbs as much as possible on his feet, using his arms only when forced to, and relying on his highly trained sense of balance for his safety. In this way insecure holds are pressed back into place, and not, as would be the case if his fingers were pulling outwards and downwards, being dragged from it. But the fallacy of the heave-and-up-we-go theory is obvious on the Hundred-Foot, for no man relying solely on his arms for propulsion could possibly reach the top without complete exhaustion overtaking him. It is too big. Only by " walking " up it can strength be conserved.

So, although the pitch was so steep that all I could

see of Hamish was the soles of his boots and two disarticulated arms, he was able to balance his way up, treading delicately, and seldom resorting to a long pull with his arms. This was as well, for I was directly below him, and the wall was loose. I was tied to a tiny spike of rock thirty feet up, and could actually see daylight between his stomach and the cliff. He took his time about it and did not send down a single stone. I followed, made myself secure, and started to bring up Hugh.

The turf ledge where I was standing was sunny and warm, and it was so pleasant to stand there, taking in the slack of the rope as Hugh advanced, and admiring the magnificent rock architecture which soared all around, that I did not immediately notice that there was no more slack to take in. Hugh at this stage was roughly half-way up, and was, by the evidence of the rope, stuck. He was out of sight. It occurred to me suddenly that he had not moved for at least five minutes.

" Anything wrong ? " I shouted.

" No," he replied. " I'm just resting. My arms have given out."

" What did he say ? " asked Hamish, firmly ensconced at the far end of a difficult forty-foot traverse.

" Arms have given out," I said. " In the name of Heaven, Hamish, I thought you said he could climb."

" I thought he could," said Hamish.

We left it at that for the moment. I kept the strain on the rope, and eventually a perspiring but absolutely unflustered Hugh was standing beside me.

" Sorry I've been so long," he said. " Grand climb this, isn't it ? "

" Grand," I said. " Look here, Hugh, how long have you been climbing ? "

Hugh seemed a little surprised at this question.

" Three or four years," he said.

" Where ? "

" The Cairngorms."

The Cairngorms are smooth, rounded mountains where a man might climb all his life without touching difficult rock.

" How many rock-climbs have you done ? " I asked.

" Two," said Hugh, " but don't you think we ought to be getting on ? I say, it *is* a grand climb. I'm enjoying this."

" Yes . . . yes, of course," I said a little weakly. " I say, Hugh, would you mind going on the middle of the rope ? Just a formality, you know, but you haven't had quite so much experience as . . . eh . . . we thought you had, and . . . eh . . . Well, please tie on the middle, anyway."

We crossed the traverse in good order, with Hugh held from both sides ; and for the next two or three pitches I watched him closely. It was a fascinating study. Beyond doubt he was destined to be an extremely useful climber, for he was without nerves. Height did not disconcert him, nor did any of the difficulties which came his way. If, as happened frequently, he was puzzled, he just kept scrabbling away until he got up. Here, clearly, was a man to whom physical fear meant very little. But he was clumsy, as nearly all beginners are. He used his arms too much, he chose the wrong holds, he moved slowly and diligently like a tank in places where tank technique

was fatal.   He was the most fantastic mixture of cold
nerve and incompetence I ever hope to see.   And he was
enjoying himself hugely.

At length we came to a place which it is necessary
to describe in some detail.   Again there was a sheer
step rising from the bed of the gully and blocking all
further progress ;   and splitting it from top to bottom
was a deep cleft.   This cleft was roofed in at the top like
an immensely elongated cave seventy feet high and only
five feet wide.   Obviously, the problem was not so
much to climb the cleft as to manœuvre somehow
outwards from underneath the roof until it was possible
to clamber on top of it, like climbing from the upper
window of a house, out and round the gutter on the
roof-edge, and so to the slates.   Just, as it were, to add
to the interest of the occasion, a lusty young waterfall
was pouring over the edge of the roof, spreading as it
fell into a fan of glittering diamonds.

" Where are your ten dry days now ? " I asked.

" I was a bit too clever," said Hamish, glowering
at the waterfall, which somehow did not look so
beautiful as it might in other circumstances have done.
" I forgot there would still be snow on the top.   The
sun hasn't dried the Chasm : it's melted the blasted
snow ! Well, here goes."

He clutched his jacket tightly round his neck and
plunged through the fall to the inner recesses of the cave.
When we joined him we found ourselves in a square
vertical chimney, with three walls of rock and one of
water.   Sixty feet above us was the roof.   Everything
was very wet and slippery.   Hamish started to climb,
using a method I had not seen before and have not seen
since : he placed his hands on one wall and his feet on

the other, thereafter walking up on the palms of his hands and the soles of his boots like a monstrous and noisy spider spinning, in a spirited imitation of the Indian rope trick, its single strand of web from floor to ceiling.

Fortunately (the climb would not have been possible otherwise) the walls of the cleft projected somewhat beyond the roof, so that before he had gained much height Hamish was able, babbling of mermaids the while, to work his way through the waterfall and out into the open air once more. We watched him through the sparkling curtain as he crawled diagonally upwards and outwards until the chimney narrowed and he was able, at last, to place one foot on each wall. By this time he was level with the edge of the roof. He waved to us once as he straddled the chimney; and then, gathering himself, heaved himself over on to one wall, crept round a corner, and disappeared from sight. He had solved the problem by avoiding the roof completely. Ten minutes later he announced that he was up and secure.

At that moment the Fates ceased to bless us, and one of the unhappier periods of my life began. For thirty minutes I employed myself in heaving the even-tempered Hugh ten feet on his journey up the chimney, and then, as he climbed beyond my reach, watching him come unstuck and dangle floorwards once more. He did not seem to mind, but I did: it was my shoulders he stood on. And so, not knowing that easy escapes from the Chasm above and below this pitch would have allowed us to walk round the obstacle, I evolved a completely preposterous plan of campaign.

I had read that, although one man could not haul

another man bodily upwards on a rope, two men sometimes could. Therefore, I said, let me go next, and Hamish and I shall pull you to the top. Hugh, not knowing any better, agreed ; and off I went.

Everything went beautifully until I reached the place where Hamish had straddled the chimney, at which point I was practically rent in twain, for, being much shorter in the leg than Hamish, I was in the attitude commonly adopted by can-can dancers at the close of their act. This, obviously, would not do at all. With the best will in the world I could not heave myself over the gap until both feet were on the far wall.

I was level with Hamish, by this time standing twelve feet away on top of the roof. As these twelve feet meant a twenty-four-foot pendulum if I came off, I was loathe to do anything ; but incipient cramp in one leg made it imperative that I do something quickly. I chose the one way open to me. I began to work my way back into the chimney, hoping to obtain some hold on the edge of the roof and to clamber over it, waterfall or no waterfall. The one great advantage of this scheme was that every foot I could wriggle towards Hamish meant two feet less to swing if I should fall.

I was level with the lip of the water and three feet from it when I slipped. My hand was within eight inches of the hold which would have taken me to the top. I parted company with the spray-wet rock, swung into the waterfall, and there remained, touching nothing and spinning slowly, for what seemed to me to be a very long time.

It really was quite a little waterfall ; but, as one half of it struck the crown of my head and the other half the gap between my neck and my collar, it was quite big enough for anything short of actual drowning, and soon my clothes were full and bulging. If I had had any sense I should have shouted to Hamish and asked him to lower me back to Hugh, sixty feet below ; but I had passed the bounds of sense. I felt and acted like a spoiled child who has been deprived of something he wants very badly. That is to say, if there had been a floor available I should probably have drummed my heels on it and screamed. As it was, there being no floor within sixty feet, I lost my temper and wasted much energy in clawing my way back on to the wall twice and being washed back off it twice, despite the fact that any person in his right mind would have seen that neither of these attempts could possibly have been successful.

After that I lost interest in the proceedings, retired to my waterfall, and began to spin again ; whereupon Hamish, receiving no intelligible answer to his requests for information and growing tired of supporting me indefinitely, lowered me towards the arms of Hugh, revolving in stately circles and gouting water in all directions. Hugh, weak with laughter, laid me out in a corner to drain.

III

The temptation to say " I told you so " is strong on any occasion when one has been wise before the event ; but in the case of the Chasm *débacle* it is irresistible. I told them in terms which left no doubts as to my views. I told them not once but many times. I argued myself into an evil temper, and still they would not listen. It was a very acrimonious argument indeed.

It started quietly enough. While I had been grubbing in the chimney, Hugh had discovered an easy escape on to the open slopes outside the Chasm ; and, after I had been lowered, Hamish had found a similar escape above the chimney. We foregathered on a convenient tussock of heather, delved into a rucksack for the guidebook, and began to discuss ways and means.

Three facts seemed to me important. First, I was soaked to the skin, utterly exhausted, and incapable of climbing farther up a route with any pretensions to difficulty. Second, although the guidebook recorded several escapes from the Chasm, the one Hamish had just climbed was the last : if we climbed any higher, we were committed to the Devil's Cauldron. And third, Hamish and Hugh had no right to carry on alone : the Cauldron, said the guidebook, was " considerably more difficult than anything yet encountered " and I was certain that Hugh would not be able to climb it.

The credit for this sober statement of the case must go to my cold douche, which had reduced me to a strictly factual view of affairs. The fine fires of enthusiasm were quenched : I could look on climbing as a centenarian looks on love, impersonally. And it seemed to me that an attempt on the Cauldron by Hamish and Hugh alone would be gratuitous folly. I said as much.

" Och, nonsense ! " said Hamish, flushed with victory and with reserves of energy still untapped, " Hugh's climbing marvellously."

" For a beginner he's climbing miraculously," I said, " but he's still a beginner."

" But, dash it, with the three of us we can do it easily. Why don't you . . ."

" Hamish," I said, " I'm done, and you know it. If it was just the wet clothes I wouldn't mind ; but it's going to take me all my time to get back to the tent. I'm sunk. I'm going back down, and I'm catching the four o'clock 'bus for home. You can take that as settled."

" We'll go on alone, then. I don't see why . . ."

The argument raged interminably. At last Hamish turned to Hugh.

" What do you say ? " he asked. " I leave it to you."

Hugh beamed.

" I'm going on," he said. " I wouldn't miss this for anything ! "

There was nothing more to be said. I left them at one o'clock, caught the 'bus, and spent an anxious evening at home, waiting for a telephone call which did not come. Next morning they still had not telephoned me, and by lunch time I had arranged for three car-loads of climbers to set off for Glencoe the minute our offices closed at night. At four o'clock the telephone rang. I lifted the receiver.

" Absolutely great ! " said a voice.

IV

Hamish's story of his adventures in the Devil's Cauldron and of the events which followed was told to me later in the week with a wealth of gesture and much laughter. It was, according to him, an enormous joke ; but, as I knew that his sense of humour would stretch to making comedy of *Hamlet*, I took the trouble to obtain Hugh's version of the tale. The result was a superb example of skill and endurance. Hamish, having allowed Hugh to walk into a mess, had made certain that he would emerge from it in safety ; and emerged in safety he had, though before this desirable end had been attained he had been in the Chasm seventeen hours.

At first everything had gone well, for the three steps above the chimney were not unduly difficult and the party, having one member less, was more mobile than it had been before. Shortly after three o'clock they stood on the floor of the Cauldron, gazing up at the 175-foot barrier which lay between them and the end of the climb. It was a grim place. No sunlight penetrated to it. They were penned in a well of sheer rock, damp and cold. Also, it was imperative that a stance be found half-way up the cliff, for Hamish had insisted that I take one of our ropes home with me, and they had only one hundred feet left.

" There was a wee cave ninety feet up," said Hamish, " a comic wee thing about the size of an arm-chair. You could just sit in it, with your legs dangling over the edge ; but there was a spike at the back where you could tie on. The climb up to it was terrific . . . A.P. if ever anything was . . . and by the time I'd hauled old Hughie up to it I was about done. Damned tiring place, the Chasm. Maybe you noticed that.

" The next bit was supposed to be the worst . . . what the guidebook calls the crux. There was a wide crack running up the wall . . . it was almost a chimney, but I couldn't quite get inside it . . . and the snag was to get out of the cave into the crack, and out of the top of the crack on to something I couldn't see.

" I got into it all right . . . at least, I got my

hands and feet in, with the seat of my pants sticking a mile outside . . . but could I get out at the top ? Could I blazes ! You never saw anything like it. But in the end I managed to get my *foot* on a knob I was using as a *hand*-hold . . . it was about level with my ear . . . and stood up on it. Talk about high kicking ! And that landed me on a sort of imaginary ledge below a slab."

This, he said, was the real crux of the climb. The slab was steep and smooth, and water was running down it. There appeared to be no holds of any kind, and no matter how he searched he could find nothing. This was serious, for he had not the slightest chance of climbing back into the crack, and there was a vertical drop of more than a hundred feet below him.

" In the end," he said, " I noticed a toe-scraping about two inches above this so-called ledge I was on. It was just a shallow scoop, a sort of faith-and-friction hold ; but when I stood on it, the extra two inches just allowed me to get one finger into a thimble-hold at the top of the slab. I got up on that, and don't ask me how I did it. I don't know. My stomach muscles are still sore.

" The rest of the route was difficult ; but after the slab it was like walking along Sauchiehall Street. I got up . . ."

Hugh said that Hamish lay at the top for five minutes before he was able to shout that he was safe, but that after another ten minutes had so far recovered as to announce that the climb was easy (" Absolutely toffee ! " was, I think, the expression used), that Hugh would have no difficulty, and that he could hold an elephant with ease from this finest of all stances.

The time was then 5.30, and the situation looked unpromising. Hugh was seated in the rock arm-chair with his feet swinging free over ninety feet of air : Hamish was eighty-five feet above him, standing in a wide chimney, able to walk about freely, and separated from the end of the climb by only twenty feet of easy scrambling. Between them lay the rope and some of the most difficult rock-climbing to be found in these islands.

All attempts to hoist the unfortunate Hugh from his little cave into the crack were unavailing. Time after time he fell off and dangled, and time after time he returned patiently to the cave to recover his wind. At last he announced calmly that he was not going to try again.

" Nothing short of a derrick will ever get me out of here," he declared. " Sorry, Hamish ; but that's the way it is."

Hamish groaned.

" Are you quite comfortable ? " he yelled.

" Yes. Fine. I'm safe as houses."

" Well, sit tight and don't move. I'm going up to the top to see if there's anyone about."

He untied, gave the rope two turns round a boulder, knotted it, and set off for the summit of Buachaille. Soon Hugh heard him in the distance, howling like a banshee. After a time the noise ceased ; and half an hour later various scrapes and clatters announced his return.

" Are you still there, Hugh ? "

" Yes."

" Still quite comfortable ? "

" Yes."

" You'd better be.   There isn't a soul on Buachaille that I can see.   I'll have to go down to Kingshouse for help."

As one was vertically above the other, it was possible to untie Hugh's end of the rope and use it to lower food and spare sweaters to him before he tied on again.   After much squirming he donned the sweaters, settled himself comfortably, and opened the guidebook.

" Righto, Hamish," he called.   " I'll read till you come back."

Five minutes later he was alone.

V

Buachaille Etive Mor is 3,345 feet high, and to climb it once in a day by its simplest route is sufficient to stretch anyone's muscles.   To climb it by way of the Chasm, with its 1,500 feet of continuously difficult rock, is to ensure extreme tiredness even if one has not had to haul two companions bodily after one.   But to climb it under these circumstances and thereafter reascend it all almost from bottom to top calls for stamina of a superlative order.   That was what Hamish set out to do.

The journey back to the tent occupied two hours : he was tired, and the route was complicated and rough ; but once in camp he imagined the worst of his troubles were over.   There he had an ancient wreck of a motor-cycle ; and, given some mountaineering guests at Kingshouse Inn, the rest should have been simple.   But there were no guests of any kind at Kingshouse ; and, as hotel maids are not the best recruits for rescue parties, he had to set off once again.

He tried Dan Mackay's barn.   It was empty.

Dan gave him an old climbing-rope someone had left in his house, and sent him off in the direction of a crofter, reputed to have two husky sons, who lived farther down the glen. It was while he was blinding down the road in the direction of this croft that he met the bakers.

They were on a motor-cycle. Hamish saw them coming and braked hard ; and when they approached he was standing in the middle of the road waving his arms, a wild, pale figure almost dropping with nervous and physical exhaustion. They saw before he spoke that something was badly wrong (Dan Mackay told me later that he looked like a ghost when he knocked at his door) ; and when he had explained the position they jumped at the chance of helping. They were bakers, they said, heading back for Glasgow to start work at four o'clock in the morning. They had time to burn. They had never been on a mountain in their lives, recognized this as a grave oversight on their part, and welcomed the opportunity of rectifying it. Where did they start ?

" In Glen Etive," said Hamish. " Follow my bike."

By ten o'clock they were at the foot of the Chasm, divesting themselves of those curious diving-suits with which motor-cyclists are wont to clothe themselves, and thereby removing much of the bulk which Hamish had taken to be brawn and muscle.

" Though, mind you, they were wiry lads," he told me, " that wasn't the trouble. The big shock I got was when one of them pointed to his gum-boots and said : " Do we go up in these ? " I said I rather thought not, so they took them off. And believe it or not they were wearing dancing pumps underneath ! "

" What did you do ? "

" Took them up in dancing pumps. What else could I do ? It was either that or bare feet, and I was desperate. And they were great, absolutely great. They climbed as if they'd been born to it. The moon was out by this time, and I took them up the south bank of the Chasm, dodged the cliffs at the top, and dropped down the screes to the edge of the wee pitch above the place where the top of the rope was.

" I was just about out of my mind with worry. I didn't wait to let them climb down to the stance. I tied the pair of them on the end of Dan's rope and lowered them down in a lump. Then I got down myself and ran to the edge. The rope was still there.

" I shouted to Hugh, and . . . gosh ! . . . I got no reply. Honest, I was nearly in tears. I shouted again, and the two bakers looked at each other as if they wondered what sort of mad-house they'd wandered into. Then Hugh replied.

" That boy's nerve is colossal ! He'd read the guidebook until it got dark, and then he'd fallen asleep. Fallen asleep ! Can you beat it ? "

That, really, is the end of the story. Hamish tied on the extra rope, keeping the bakers as far from the edge as possible (he was afraid to let them know how great a drop was below them : in the moonlight it must have looked ghastly) ; and, when all was ready, gave the order to pull. Hugh came up like a sack, for his hands were too cold to grip the rock.

" When he was six feet from the top," said Hamish, " I yelled : " One last heave ! " ; and the bakers heaved, and I heaved, and old Hughie came louping over the edge like a twelve-stone salmon. After that we lay in a heap for ten minutes and laughed till we were sore. Sort of hysterical, I suppose we were. We couldn't stop."

It was 1 a.m. They picked themselves up, reached the road, shook hands with the bakers, and made for camp. They slept until noon. By the time they had returned Dan's rope and returned to Glasgow, it was 4 p.m.

And Hugh, who worked in a bank, had the keys of the safe in his pocket.

CHAPTER FIFTEEN

ENVOI

EIGHT years ago, fresh air was still the property of moneyed men, a luxury open to the few. With a hundred faces and places fresh in my mind, I find this fact difficult to believe, yet it is true. Eight years ago there were only a few Choochters and Hamishes on the roads ; and the Highlands, where to-day the youth hostel chains link the most remote glens, were a desert of deer-stalking. Hiking was the hobby of an enthusiastic handful, and climbing was a rich man's sport. Only the cyclists had learned to escape from the cities.

Then came the hostels and lightweight tents, both of them cheap ; and now the roads are thick with week-end traffic, and in glens once deserted are hostels where the summer visitor must book in advance if he is to find a bed. In Glen Nevis, for example, there is a hostel which is one hundred miles from the nearest city and consequently stands empty most of the winter : yet each year the total number of times its beds are slept in is over six thousand. A bed in Glen Nevis in July is a thing to be prized, and the ground round the hostel is white with tents. Fresh air has become cheap.

It is unfair to make the previous chapters of this book illustrate the point, for most of the incidents described in them occurred in districts far removed from my home ; yet, even so, none of them was expensive. The hunger-march holiday in Skye lasted for a fortnight and cost me £4 from Glasgow back to Glasgow. A pound note would cover the cost of any other incident mentioned, and ten shillings was enough for most of them. I once spent a week-end in Dan Mackay's barn, eighty miles from home, with a hitch-hiker who had raided the larder before starting and had two days of first-class climbing for sixpence, which he spent on cigarettes !

But cheapness and popularity have their dangers, particularly for those who climb. The sport is growing too quickly. There was a time when no novice climbed except by invitation : it was an obscure game, contagious rather than infectious, and people took to rock and snow because they had friends who were addicts. The itch was transmitted by personal contact, and first ascents were supervised by competent leaders.

But now it is an infectious disease, a something in the air, contracted by people who have no leader to help them over the dangerous learning period. They go to a hostel. They see people, strangely booted and swathed in ropes, setting off for the hills. Then one day they find themselves walking up a hill by an easy route, and, coming on a cliff and remembering what they saw at the hostel, decide that this might be a sport worth investigating. They investigate it. They have unnailed boots, no rope, no experience ; but they investigate it. And next morning the newspapers have the same old story to tell.

The number of fatal mountaineering accidents in Scotland has more than trebled during the past three years ; and, almost without exception, those killed have been novices. This is wicked waste of life. There is no excuse for it, for clubs exist which are willing to train new members ; and, even if clubs were not available, theoretical knowledge gained from books is safeguard against the more flagrant errors, and might easily have reduced the recent death-roll by half. Few people imagine that they can buy their first set of golf clubs and break seventy on a first-class course within a week ; but a surprising number buy their first boots and set off to climb the north face of Buachaille in winter.*

I do not preach without experience. I was just as stupid myself.

II

It is customary for writers of books in which mountaineering is mentioned to explain at this stage why they commit the safety of their necks and limbs to inhospitable crags ; why, by deliberate choice, they freeze in gullies, alarm their relatives, suffer wind, rain, hail, sleet, and snow, parch themselves on waterless ridges, dress like scarecrows, squander their substance on ropes and railway fares, eat seldom, and fill the kitchen Monday after Monday with a collection of soaked and odorous rags.

It is vain, against such accumulated evidence, to say that one meets such nice people, or that there was a pretty view on top, or even that one just happens to like climbing. So inadequate did any argument appear to the pioneers of the Alps, where mountaineering was born, that they disguised themselves as scientists and battled their way up Mont Blanc weighed down by

*These remarks apply even more forcefully in these post-war days. The accident rate has been rising steadily year by year. Most of the victims are still non-climbers.

barometers for measuring the altitude, tinted cards to tell posterity precisely how blue the sky was on top, and pistols to explode the theory that sound behaved in an unorthodox manner at 15,000 feet. Each and all of these experiments was completely fatuous ; but no doubt they were the most convincing ones the pioneers could think of on the spur of the moment. Not until the seventies of last century, when Leslie Stephen wrote *The Playground of Europe*, did mountaineers dare to admit that they climbed for the sheer love of climbing. They have been bogged ever since in a morass of psychology, metaphysics, and physiology, floundering in search of concrete arguments wherewith to convert the heathen to the sanity and sweet reasonableness of climbing.

They have been unsuccessful, and always will be. Tibetans, seeing the yak-train of an Everest expedition approach, nudge each other and remark that these foreigners must either be seeking gold, or suffering from delusions. The Briton, with his superior knowledge of metallurgy, inclines to the second of these conclusions. Climbing is incomprehensible, and therefore silly. And, moreover, it is dangerous. If it is pointed out to a golfer that nothing of ethical or practical value accrues from propelling a ball round a curiously farmed field into eighteen cavities decorated with flags, he snorts and says :

" But that's different. I don't run the risk of breaking my neck."

And with the air of having squashed the argument once and for all, he goes out and plays another round.

That is the Man in the Street's argument, and he will not budge from it however ingenious the arguments advanced by mountaineers. It is reasonable, and, indeed, praiseworthy, to play bridge, darts, pontoon, ludo, billiards, tennis, shove ha'-penny, dominoes; to solve crossword puzzles and acrostics; collect stamps and ancient coins; pay a shilling to boo at football or sleep at cricket; perform any of the hundred and one exercises by which mankind seeks to divert itself. But you must not break your neck. You must play safe, take care of yourself, keep your feet dry and your throat well wrapped up against the night air.

I shall break my neck if I choose; but I have no intention of doing so. Mountaineering, whatever the Man in the Street may think, is not a dangerous sport unless it is embarked upon without knowledge, though it would be idle to contend that accidents, serious accidents, cannot happen. They do happen. Experienced climbers have been killed. In Scotland an experienced man is killed roughly once every two years. But, even considering the relatively small number of people engaged in it, climbing is still a safer sport than motoring, and the risk of unavoidable disaster is so slight as to be negligible. There is, in other words, just enough risk in the game to make it attractive without being foolhardy. It may appear to some that an undue number of risks are related in this book; but it must be remembered that risky days make more interesting reading than those when everything goes according to plan. Out of scores of climbs I can think of only one not related in this book during which I ran any appreciable risk of injury.

I climb—the Man in the Street will still shake his head, but I follow my masters and try to explain—for many reasons, some obvious, some not, all blending and playing their part in this urge which takes people to the hills. The urge defies analysis ; but many of its components are within the range of ordinary human experience, as, for example, the attraction of beauty and unexpected strangeness which may lie round any corner on a mountain.

One may climb through dense mist and emerge above a sea of clouds stretching endlessly and unbroken to the horizon ; or find a green translucent pool, warm as milk and made for bathing, among the rocks ; or see a boulder-strewn hillside converted by the magic of mist into a petrified forest more terrible than the fears of childhood, yet friendly because it is understood. And again, climbing is a sport demanding skill, and as such is satisfying. And again, it gives one friends of a peculiarly intimate kind : one does not put one's life in the hands of an acquaintance.

But to my mind it finds its chief justification as an antidote for modern city life, where we live on wheels and use our bodies merely as receptacles for our brains. Many people rate against city life ; but I must confess that it suits me very well. It exercises my brain. It also fills my brain, as it fills the brains of everyone, with a multitude of petty worries, agile little fellows who even during my leisure prick my memory and conscience.

One cannot sweat and worry simultaneously. The mountain resolves itself into a series of simple problems, unconfused by other issues. Abstractions are foreign to it : its problems are solid rock, to be wrestled with physically ; and in the sheer exuberance of thinking through his fingers and toes as his primaeval fathers did before him the climber's worries vanish, sweated from his system, leaving his brain free to appreciate beauty, which is never petty and never troubled anyone who understood it.

And so it is, to a greater or lesser degree, with the hikers and the cyclists, for how else can be explained the miles which spin behind wheels and crawl from dusty shoes ? Something of value is on the roads and hills, and thousands set out each Saturday to find it. Each one sees it differently. I have only described what I have found.